Suddenly, Jaynie noticed her reflection and Liz's playing in the shimmering circles of water. Their heads seemed to bob back and forth, closer together and then separating. Liz's on the right, and her own on the left, together, apart, together, apart. Or *was* that her own reflection? It had to be, and yet it didn't look exactly right, wiggled out of shape by the ripples. Of course it was! She was on the left, Liz was on the right, and—and the one in— She blinked and shook her head.

The face in the middle!! Between them!!

Jaynie shut her eyes tightly and opened them as wide as she could. Yes, there was a *third* face! In between them! And its cold eyes never blinked—it was the stare of the dead!

# Deadly Sleep

## Dale Cowan

LAUREL-LEAF
BOOKS

Published by
Dell Publishing
a division of
Bantam Doubleday Dell Publishing Group, Inc.
666 Fifth Avenue
New York, New York 10103

The trademark Laurel-Leaf Library® is registered in the U.S.
Patent and Trademark Office.

The trademark Dell® is registered in the U.S. Patent and
Trademark Office.

ISBN: 0-440-91961-4

RL: 6.1

Printed in the United States of America

One Previous Edition

October 1992

10  9  8  7  6

# Chapter One

"Are you dead?"

"I feel dead." Jaynie's throat tightened as she wondered why it wasn't getting dark. No one had told her the light would last so long, hanging on almost unendingly, giving up its life so painfully slowly, so unnaturally.

"I've never felt anything like this before. It's so creepy! Will the whole night be—like *this?*" she asked in amazement, hoping Evelyn or her father would tell her otherwise. She wanted the dark, she wanted the night, she wanted to sleep.

"No, lass," Mr. David Macdonald answered, a faint smile on his lips. "The Scottish gloaming, as we call it, only lasts till about ten-thirty in the

1

summertime, and it's already ten-fifteen, mind you. Soon it'll be getting dark."

Jaynie looked through the car window, into the dark green countryside where flocks of sheep huddled, as if to protect themselves against the threat of night before it closed in on them.

"Well, when will the sun rise?" she asked.

"Oh, I dare say you'll not be up to see it," answered Mr. Macdonald, "but the sky will brighten around four o'clock. We're so far north that the summer nights are extremely short. You'll have to learn how to sleep very fast," he teased.

Evelyn leaned forward and said, "Don't worry, Jaynie, tomorrow you can sleep as late as you want. How many hours now have you been up?"

"I left Cincinnati at, well, I can't remember how long it's been. I know the time changed somewhere over Greenland, but I must have missed a couple of hours. My watch says one-fifteen. Let's just say I've been up for over twenty hours and you'll probably have one sleepy guest, dead for a few days from a severe case of jetlag." Evelyn had a quick playful vision of hanging a mourning wreath on their front door.

Jaynie *was* exhausted, but not only from the jetlag. She had spent the entire plane ride thinking about her recent breakup with Tim. Unable to think about the wonderful summer ahead of her, she had sat there brooding about the past. There had been a young couple, obviously in love, sitting across the aisle from her and she had watched them out of the corner of her eye. The more she

2

had watched them, the more upset and angry she got, because they reminded her so much of how things had been with Tim before he had gone to California and met that other girl.

Now, as she peered through the car window, she tried to lose herself in the scenery, hoping the anger would melt away. She stared at the countryside as the little car reeled around the bends and curves in the road. She had never seen such a softly rolling land, studded with dark trees and flocks of sheep; the uncertain cast of the evening sky set everything off, as if it were some fairyland. The world of real objects seemed to be fading in that glow, dissolving into something dark, colorless and featureless. Jaynie's head was spinning, probably from lack of sleep, she thought. It was more and more difficult to keep her mind on what Evelyn and her dad were talking about.

"Well," she yawned. "I would love to see some castles while I'm here. Do they let people go through them?"

"Ay, but not the ones that are haunted," answered Mr. Macdonald laughing. "It's far too terrifying."

"Daddy, don't start your ghost routine on Jaynie so early. Give her a few days to get settled," said Evelyn. She turned to Jaynie, happy to announce her big news. "You may get to see a castle tomorrow."

"Tomorrow?" Jaynie couldn't believe that the very next day she'd get a look at the medieval past she had read and studied about in school. It was as if her Scottish friend had said, "When we go around this bend in the road, we'll be back in 1066."

"Yep. My friend, Liz Beattie, and her brother, Brian—who, by the way, is really eager to meet you—have invited us to go with them to visit an old castle in Fife. Their father owns it."

"*Owns* it?" She felt wide awake now and was surprised to think that anyone actually owned a castle anymore. Castles were more like museums or tourist attractions that made postcards of Britain look so romantic and mysterious. "Owns it?" she asked again. "What do you mean? Are they the descendants of lords or a noble family?"

"Hardly," explained Evelyn, giggling. "They *are* loaded, though. The Beatties are one of the largest landowners in the region. How much property do they have, Daddy?"

"Oh, I might guess ten thousand acres. Maybe a wee bit more. Most of it's pastureland for cattle and sheep."

"It's the old Fermleven estate up in Fife," Evelyn continued. "It's been empty for generations, just sort of rotting there. Mr. Beattie is one of the leading Scottish preservationists, so he bought it a few years ago. They've been restoring it and are just about ready to open it to the public for tours. Brian says that his dad even wants to let outside groups rent the banquet hall for weddings and parties. It's so gorgeous, you can't imagine."

"And," teased Jaynie, poking Mr. Macdonald gently with her elbow, "did they drive out all the

4

ghosts so the tourists wouldn't be scared?"

"Well, now, Jaynie, you're asking me questions that I don't rightly know a lot about. However, knowing Ian Beattie, I'd say he's left one or two friendly ghosts to add to the historic atmosphere of the estate. He'd want the tourists to get the full Scottish experience, you know." He paused to emphasize "full" and "Scottish." "On the other hand, if the ghosts demanded certain 'haunting privileges' that included the right to scare un-suspecting—"

"Daddy!" Evelyn interrupted him. "Ignore him, Jaynie."

"Now, Evie, you know that Britain has a well-deserved reputation as the Land of Ghosts. We're supposed to have more ghosts and haunted places than any other nation in the world."

"Ay, Mr. Macdonald. I wouldna wanna meet oop with one." Suppressing a smile and a giggle, she tried hard to fake a proper Scottish accent and keep a straight face. She thought she had mas-tered it quite well, having listened to Evelyn for the past year. In fact, Evelyn had everyone in Jaynie's family rolling their r's and emphasizing the melody of syllables. When Evelyn first arrived in America as an exchange student, Jaynie's family joked about making her feel at home, and they all did their best to imitate the soothing Scottish accent. Now Evelyn was making Jaynie feel at home.

The car suddenly lurched around a treacherous bend in the road and was swallowed up in an unusually thick patch of fog. Somewhere out there was the promise of adventure. Jaynie could feel it. It was pulling her into the heart of Scotland, calling her to a summer that would be like no other in her life. Jaynie had looked forward to this day for months, since February, when Evelyn had invited her. She read up on Scottish history and geography and asked Evelyn to tell her all about Scottish customs. She even memorized old Scottish ballads that she found particularly enchanting. Somewhere behind that blanket of moist gauze was Scotland—castles, storybook villages, a whole new world, waiting out there in the fog, waiting to spring upon her, and change her.

"It's like being blindfolded and led into some strange place where I can't get my bearings," said Jaynie.

"You'll be snuggling up in front of the fire in a few minutes," assured Evelyn. "We're in Tweedkeith, now. We're almost home."

They drove down streets and lanes bordered with shops and homes, unrecognizable in the fog. Finally, they turned onto Queen Street, then onto the pebbled driveway alongside the Macdonald's small stone house. When they got out of the car, Jaynie noticed that the Scottish night was chilly. The fog thinned for a moment, and she confronted the dark, ominous outline of a large hill, looming up into the night sky like a great black beast lurking on the horizon.

"Look at that!" she whispered.

"Ronan's Hill," said Evelyn, smiling. "Enormous, isn't it?"

Suddenly, a yellow light flashed on behind her. She turned and saw Evelyn's mother standing in the doorway. Jaynie stepped onto the porch and said, "Hi!"

"Well Jaynie Gerard! Come in and warm yourself by the fire." Smiling, she held out her arms to Jaynie and gave her a tight motherly hug and kissed her cheek. "You must be exhausted from your long journey." Betty Macdonald held her arm protectively around Jaynie's shoulder and led her through the door and down a dim, narrow hallway. She went into a bright cheerful room, lit with softly burning lamps and the welcoming glow of a coal fire.

"Umm, it feels good in here," said Jaynie, unzipping her jacket and stretching out on the rug.

Mrs. Macdonald left the room and returned shortly, carrying a tray with three mugs of steaming hot chocolate. Each girl grabbed a cup and began sipping. Jaynie closed her eyes as she let the hot steam rise up on her face.

Evelyn's mother pulled up a chair and said, "Now, Jaynie, I imagine David has talked your ear off on the trip from Glasgow, so I'll not be asking you very much tonight. You need to rest up and get over your jetlag. But, mind you, I want to know all about you and your family. Evelyn's been telling us a lot about you. We're very happy you're here, and we hope you like it well enough to stay all summer."

Jaynie felt good and at home. She felt relaxed and sleepy from the fire and hot chocolate. She gazed into the firey bed of coals, suddenly realizing that she had made it to Scotland. She looked out the window, but all she saw was the fog, swirling under the streetlamps. Out there were the green glens and dark hills she had just traveled through, with their heather, and ancient castles. Maybe even ghosts. She shivered with anticipation. How far away that was, another land, a place far behind her. She was on her own now. Away from Ohio, away from school, away from Tim and the fresh memories of how he had hurt her. She hoped the summer in Scotland would help her to forget him. If nothing else happens here, she thought, it will be wonderful to stop thinking about Tim once and for all.

Evelyn interrupted their shared silence.

"Had enough chocolate, Jaynie?" She too was getting tired. "Let me show you to your room."

# Chapter Two

As she got ready for bed, Jaynie noticed a prayer written in needlepoint, framed and hanging over the bookshelf. It read:

Ancient Scottish Prayer—
From ghoulies and ghosties
And long-legged beasties
And things that go bump in the night,
Good Lord, deliver us.

"Jaynie!" a voice whispered. The door cracked open a few inches and Evelyn's face peeked in. "I saw your light on under the door and thought I'd see if everything is all right."

"Oh, thanks, Evelyn. Everything's great. Your

parents are terrific. I think I'm going to really like them."

"And they like you already," assured Evelyn. "I'm just across the hall and Mum and Dad are down at the end, if you need anything. Is this room okay?"

"It's fine. It looks like it's collected a lot of interesting stuff over the years. Have a lot of visitors slept here before me?"

"You better believe it. Mum likes to have guests. You aren't the first to sleep in this bed." Jaynie let her gaze roam around the room again, her eyes stopping suddenly at the collection of enlarged photographs arranged just a few feet above where she lay.

"Those photographs are really odd." She sat up to see them better. They were black and white, and, she noticed, each was out of focus. Why would the Macdonalds hang such unprofessional photos in the guest room? "What are they supposed to be?" she asked, leaning closer to the wall to get a better look.

"Oh, those." Evelyn made a face. "Liz Beattie took them. It's her hobby. When I left for the States last year, she gave them to me to remind me of Scotland. But they were so depressing I left them here, and Daddy hung them up. Don't pay any attention to them. Scotland's nothing like Liz's pictures."

"They're creepy. It's hard to see exactly what's going on in them."

There were five blown-up photographs in

wooden frames, each looking like it had either been taken in the rain or mist, or overexposed.

"What are they pictures of?" Jaynie repeated her question. They weren't pleasing photos.

"I'm not sure. I didn't want to hurt Liz's feelings by asking. I may as well tell you about Liz before you meet her tomorrow." She thought of how she wanted to put it. "Liz has been extremely moody and depressed for quite some time. I think she still sees a doctor in Edinburgh. We had been best friends in primary school, but ever since we got to high school, she's been more and more out of it, living in her own little world, without much interest in anything. Sometimes she really depresses me. Mum wrote last year that Liz had gotten worse since I went to America. But I know it's not only because she *missed* me, because we just weren't that close in recent years. We drifted apart, or—" Evelyn paused to reconsider. "—Or *she* sort of drifted off."

Evelyn leaned across the bed with a sad expression on her tired face. "This, I think, is Ronan's Hill, the big one that frightened you," she said, pointing to the lower left photo. "These two seem to be of the same tree taken in the fog, but from different angles. It must be winter since there aren't any leaves on it. I always think those two bare limbs are the arms of a skeleton. I don't know what that one up there is, but it looks like the turret of a castle with a cloud behind it."

"But the one in the middle. Boy, is that spooky." Jaynie was looking at a photo that

11

depicted a large rock in the lower third of the picture. The rock had a rough, blurred border that seemed to be two or three edges intertwined. Above it was an area with swirling layers of light and dark, a marbled effect, but strongly suggesting depth and an emptiness that one could fall into, like a coiled pit descending far down into nothingness.

"That is the only one I know for sure," said Evelyn. "It's Fiona's Rock out at Fermleven, the Beattie's estate in Fife where we're going tomorrow. It was taken from the top of the rock looking down, maybe thirty feet, into the water below."

"But why is it so blurry? Does Liz always take her photos in this weird summer twilight?"

"No," laughed Evelyn. "Sometimes I think Liz takes double exposures to give her pictures that eerieness she seems to like so much." She paused. "Notice something even stranger about this one?"

She watched her friend's face, to see what her reaction would be. Jaynie moved closer to the photo. It just looked like a blurry rock with murky water beneath it.

"No, I—what do you mean? It's just—" Then she saw it. "Wait a minute! Oh, Evie, is there really something there? Do you mean—?"

"Ay, in the water. Look closely. It helps if you look a little to the side."

"It's a *figure*. In a white robe. Isn't it? A person under water! Is it a dead body? Or just a double exposure?"

"Well," sighed Evelyn. "*I* think it's a double exposure but it's supposed to be a ghost."

"A ghost?"

"Liz claims she caught the spirit of Fiona, the Highland princess who commited suicide by jumping off this rock centuries ago. It's an old legend and all I know about it is that Lady Fiona jumped from the rock into Loch Ferm, the lake, and drowned, when she discovered that her lover had been murdered."

"Her lover was *murdered?*" Jaynie interrupted. "How terrible! I can't imagine how awful that must be to have your—" Her voice broke off suddenly as she realized that she knew exactly how it would feel. Tim wasn't dead, of course, but he may as well have been. Jaynie shivered. She could certainly identify with this Lady Fiona legend.

"And she—" Jaynie hesitated to say the word. "And she *haunts* the castle we're going to tomorrow?"

"No, silly." Laughing, Evelyn punched her friend playfully on the shoulder. "It's not haunted. Forget what Daddy said; he was only teasing you. No one's ever reported anything supernatural at Fermleven."

"But Loch Ness has some monster or spirit in it."

"Ay, so they say," replied Evelyn skeptically.

"Are other lakes in Scotland haunted, too?"

"Some, perhaps. But don't worry. Loch Ferm is

just an old lake. There's nothing strange about it, or Fermleven." She paused in consideration. "Except, of course, Liz. But you'll find out tomorrow when you meet her." She sighed. "We used to be such good friends. Oh well, I hope her moodiness doesn't affect you. Sometimes she can be hard to take."

"Well," sighed Jaynie, snuggling up under the comforter. "'Tomorrow is another day.'"

"Right. Jaynie, I'm really glad you're here. I hope you'll enjoy your stay with us as much as I loved staying with you." She leaned over and gave her friend a pat and a hug, then turned out the lamp by the bedside. "I hope this summer is good for you Jaynie—to get over Tim, I mean. Good night. Sleep tight."

"I'm sure I will," murmured Jaynie.

She closed her eyes and listened to Evelyn leave the room and pull the door closed. It was an old door with a sturdy metal latch that clicked solidly. The room grew dark.

Finally, time to rest, to relax, she thought. If only Tim were here. No, if only she could forget him.

She arched her back a bit and slid her hands beneath the small of it. She rubbed it where it still ached. It had been an unbearably long transatlantic flight, not to mention the car ride across almost the entire breadth of Scotland. She remembered how Tim used to rub her back for her after her riding accident. She rolled over on her side to face the wall. Betty Macdonald had given her a second pillow which she now clutched snugly in the curve of her body. It made her feel secure to have it between her knees and to hug it tightly against her chest. She pushed her chin down into its fresh, clean, powdery smell, waiting for the sleep she knew would not be long in coming. She was painfully tired.

Then, just as she started to drift off, the floor creaked in the hall, outside her door, and her eyes popped open. Maybe it was one of the Macdonalds getting ready for bed, she told herself. She thought of the prayer on the wall, and sighed. About to close her eyes once more, she was suddenly aware of a light, glowing on the wall above her. Then, a disturbing feeling that it might be a light *in* the wall, or *behind* it, shining through. It had a soft, subtle glow. But it was only the streetlight spilling through the sheer curtains and splashing on the wall, illuminating Liz Beattie's dreary photos. Jaynie rolled her eyes to look up at them without taking her chin out of the pillow, without moving. Nothing looks very alive in them, she thought. They all seem like lonely, dead places.

Except for the one of Loch Ferm with its mysterious figure in the shadowy depths of the water. The photograph held her gaze, as if it had some angry, deliberate power over her. For a second, Jaynie thought she saw the hazy water in the picture ripple, as if the wind was blowing silently across it, or a menacing fog was lifting—

or even as if the bleached figure in the water was about to—

No way, she thought, it can't possibly move. I'm just exhausted.

She sat up on her elbow to examine it more closely. It moved! It did move. The princess in the photo . . . the body under the water . . . Jaynie leaned forward. How silly! She smiled with relief as she watched her own shadow dart up against the wall. She turned quickly to look out the window. Something moved outside. A shadow—a person, quickly, casting its shadow onto the photo of Loch Ferm. But this is the second floor! Her heart started to race.

She rolled over and pulled the curtains aside. There it was—a tree limb bobbing in the wind in front of the streetlamp! Jaynie lay back down and rolled over into her security pillow, her heart still pounding. She closed her eyes again, thinking that the limb was the first clear thing she'd seen outside since she'd arrived.

So much to see, she sighed, and began to relax again.

As she fell asleep, the shadow of the limb continued to bob across the lake in the photo, up and down, up and down, like some conscious thing, rising in the brackish water—slowly, deliberately, washing ashore.

# Chapter Three

Someone was calling.

"Jaaay-nieee!"

In the confused muffle of sleep, she couldn't tell whose voice it was. Could it be morning already? Again, she heard a voice, a young girl's faint, distant voice calling to her.

"Jaay-nieee!" Again, with a new urgency.

It sounded like the high-pitched squeak of a rusty-hinged door. It couldn't be Evelyn, she'd knock and then come in. It must be someone else. Who? The voice was too young to belong to Mrs. Macdonald. Jaynie opened her eyes. It was still night, not even four o'clock yet. From the corner of her eye, she could see the tree limb jerk every once in a while in the wind. The room was cold.

Then she heard it a third time: "Jaaay-nieee!" It was behind her. On the wall.

Slowly, fearfully, she rolled over onto her back, clutching her security pillow. She looked up at the photograph of Loch Ferm. It seemed a bit brighter than it had before. In fact, it glowed. No, she thought, that's crazy! And yet—it was greener! Yes, it was steadily getting brighter—*and* greener—as she lay there watching it. But how could a black and white photograph get *greener*, she wondered.

Then the watery area in the photo rippled. Just a bit.

Sure now that it wasn't the shadow from the tree limb, Jaynie propped herself up to get a better look. She blinked. The figure of the dead princess glowed brighter and sharper, more distinguishable than it had been earlier in the evening.

Once again she heard her name called. Turning back the comforter, she moved closer to the wall and knelt there. Her own shadow from the window completely covered the picture, blocking out all light from the street. Still the ghostly figure of the drowned princess glowed with a milky-green radiance that wavered eerily. The movement was either the motion of the waves on the water's surface, or ... the dead girl was somehow breathing, though she stood far down in the depths of the loch! Watery weeds and algae, twisted with the slime of rotting leaves, clung to her face, covering it, but Jaynie could see that she

18

had tilted her head back, ever so slightly, lifting her face upward, gazing at the water's surface above her.

And then her mouth opened!

A stream of iridescent bubbles emerged, floated up to the surface, and broke the top of the water.

Jaynie leaned so close to the photo that her own face was less than an inch from the glass. Her breath fogged up the cold glass as the bubbles from below burst over the surface of the loch. Far down in the depths of the water, stood the white-gowned princess, Fiona, opening and closing her mouth. Her robe and the pea green-colored weeds that wrapped and twined around her skeletal body blew as if a wet, cavernous wind engulfed her down below.

Jaynie could almost *hear* the girl breathe. In the next explosion of bubbles, she heard her name once again.

"Jaay-nieee!"

The dead princess was talking to her! Fiona *knew* her! In a quivering, weak whisper, Jaynie forced herself to answer.

"What—what do you—want?"

The reply was gurgled and unclear, as the sounds rose from the watery depths. But to Jaynie, it sounded as if the voice replied:

"All that could be found!"

Suddenly, the bright green bubbles exploded upon the surface of the loch, the water turned black, and all was motionless. The white weedy robe ceased to blow in the phantom wind, and the leafy tendrils of weeds and vines hung motionless around the girl's wet body. The stark, unnatural light that had given life to the figure in the picture gradually faded until the contrast of black and white in the photograph once again assumed its normal shading. Jaynie's head cast a smothering shadow over the photo and then the wall fell dark.

Jaynie blinked. The room was chilly and she shivered. Her hands were still placed on either side of the picture frame, palms against the wall, her nose almost touching the glass. Her warm breath fogged the glass even more. She shivered again. Then she lay back down and pulled the covers up to her chin. She looked again at the photo, now illuminated solely by the streetlight.

She shook her head to rid herself of the images dancing menacingly in her brain—the girl in the long, white robe, the weeds, the lake. The lake image began to melt, but snapped back again—this time sharper but slightly changed. A different lake, the lake back home under the high, hot sun beating down on the riding trail. And then Jaynie's horse was rearing and she was falling—grabbing for Tim. But he got further and further away, riding off without her. Jaynie clasped her head between her hands. "NO!" she thought. "Not again." It was the same dream that had been tormenting her all spring—the dream about her back injury and her breakup with Tim. Now it came spinning into focus again for the first time in weeks. Jaynie had hoped it was out of her system for good but she was helpless against its intrusion into her semi-consciousness.

Now, the dark dust of the riding path flashed alternately in Jaynie's head with the green, glimmering water of Loch Ferm. The two dreams were mixed together, the images hopelessly confused and disorienting.

"Why?" Jaynie pleaded silently. "Somebody help me." She tightly squeezed her eyes shut, then consciously relaxed them. She was terrified, confused, completely drained of energy. Despite her fright and the pounding, ominous feeling in her chest, she was soon overcome by sleep.


"I feel like I could sleep all day I tossed and turned all night," Jaynie said, as Evelyn backed the car out of the drive. They were on their way to Fermleven castle.

"Is your back still giving you trouble?" Evelyn asked. She could see Jaynie's head jerk suddenly—angrily—to look at her and then back to the road again. "Oh, I'm sorry. I wasn't thinking. Really. I know you don't want to talk about the accident, or Tim."

Jaynie felt the blood drain from her face. "Evelyn, I realize I have to get over him, and I know I can't avoid talking about him, or even thinking about him, forever. It's just, oh, I don't know."

She fell quiet and Evelyn wasn't sure what to say, or what not to say. She pointed out the distant spires in Edinburgh as they rounded a bend in the road, but Jaynie's enthusiasm was half-hearted. It would be good for her if she did talk about Tim, thought Evelyn. Why not? She needs to get things off her chest.

"Your letter arrived about a week before you 'did,'" she began, treading carefully in the water of Jaynie's injured emotions. "I really felt sorry for you."

"Oh, Evelyn, I could have killed him. I really think I could have *killed* him. I never felt so hostile toward another human being in my whole life. Men!" she snapped angrily. She pondered a moment and then went on, "I still can't stand not knowing what's really going on out there in California. At first, it had seemed so perfect. He was going back for summer classes at the university, and I was coming to Scotland, so neither of us would have to mope around Cincinnati all summer, waiting for the other. Now who knows what will happen when we both get back." Jaynie threw her hands up in the air and let them fall in her lap. "If he even *comes* back." Her voice dropped as she grew more discouraged about the future. "That's the hardest part, Evelyn. I can't even be sure he'll come back, or want to see me if he does."

"What's the name of the girl in California?"

"Julie. He didn't tell me much about her, naturally! But evidently they really hit it off when he was out there during the winter quarter, and when he came back in the spring—" She broke

22

off, her voice wavering ever so slightly. "Oh, Evie, let's not talk about it. It's just too painful, and it's putting me in a bad mood. All those weekends with him, horseback riding and sailing, and making plans for the summer, and he was exchanging all those love letters with her behind my back. Let's talk about something else. It hurts too much, like—" She couldn't find the word. "And, what's more, I get depressed to admit that I can't get over it. I think about it all the time. It's really getting to me. I feel like I'm obsessed by it."

"Sure," said Evelyn consolingly. "I want to point out some places along the way before we get to Fermleven, and also we—" She broke her train of thought abruptly, as she suddenly remembered. "You haven't told me yet about last night."

"What do you mean?"

"Your nightmare, your dream. What was it about?"

"Oh," Jaynie muttered. "I don't know. It got all mixed up with the dream I used to have about my accident and Tim. But it was weird, Evie. I didn't think any dream could be as vivid or unsettling as that accident dream, but the one last night, well, when I first woke up this morning, I almost thought it was real. I don't remember the details too well, but just thinking about it makes my head spin. You know something? At the time it seemed just like those lucid dreams we talked about in our dream club last year. You know, the ones where you *know* you're dreaming and sometimes can even control the dream." She paused a moment trying to remember it. "But now I can't even remember the details. Darn!"

"You can't remember anything?"

"I think I was drowning. Or—or murdering someone." She shook her head. "I really can't remember."

Evelyn wondered whether it was Tim she was murdering, but kept quiet about it.

"See that?" She indicated with her finger. "When we cross that long bridge, we'll be in Fife, and then, before you know it, we'll be at Fermleven, your very first castle."

"Which one is Brian?" asked Jaynie eagerly, looking down the long sweep of gravel that was the formal drive up to Fermleven Manor. In front of the old stone castle stood the two boys, looking anxiously down the drive every now and then. By the time Jaynie had asked the question, both were watching the car. The tall, curly-haired boy wearing a dark blue sweatshirt waved at them.

"The tall one who just waved," said Evelyn smiling, but with her eye on the shorter, ruddy-faced boy on the left. "And the other, of course, is Craig." She waved from inside the car, but they were close enough that the boys saw it. Craig returned her wave and broke into a broad welcoming grin.

"Good morning, Evie!" Craig came right up and

locked Evelyn in a warm hug and kiss, then turned to Jaynie. "And you must be—"

"Yes," introduced Evelyn proudly. "This *is* Jaynie Gerard from Cincinnati, but take it easy. She's going to be here all summer."

"Hi, Jaynie, I'm Brian Beattie. I've been waiting to meet you for months," announced the tall boy in the sweatshirt, with a smile that seemed to reach right out and touch her. She liked the fact that he didn't wait to be introduced. She took his hand firmly. She liked the strength and certainty in the way he held onto her own hand just a moment longer than was really necessary.

"And this," continued Evelyn, slipping her arm through Craig's, "is Craig Selkirk, whom you've heard so much about." Jaynie let go of Brian's hand and shook Craig's. She had been wanting to meet Evelyn's boyfriend for months. She had been slightly envious of all the letters that had arrived for Evelyn postmarked Scotland, all year long.

"Hi, Craig, it's nice to finally meet you."

"And this," announced Brian Beattie with a wide sweep of his arm and a sharp turn on his heel, "is Fermleven Manor. Welcome to Fermleven, Jaynie."

In the fluster of introductions, Jaynie hadn't had a chance to take a good look at the huge bulk of inert stone behind them. The massive old building seemed to expand in its width the full length of a city block, as well as in its height. Jaynie tilted her head back and looked into the gray morning sky where the turrets along the castle wall almost faded into the air, their wet gray stonework sculpted into pointed towers that could hardly be seen from down where they stood.

"It's enormous!" she exclaimed. The immense structure had the same startling effect, the same threatening presence, as Ronan's Hill had the night before. Suddenly, her eye caught a movement in an open window high on one of the rounded turrets. She thought she saw a flash of long, yellow hair, the only bright splash of color along the gray facade of the wall. Brian turned around to see what had caught Jaynie's attention.

"Oh, that's Liz, my sister. We both spent the night here so we could get ready for you. She's still up in her room."

"Spent the night?" Jaynie had thought that the Beatties lived at Fermleven Manor all the time.

"Ay, we don't live here, you know."

"I didn't tell you," explained Evelyn, "the Beatties live just outside of Tweedkeith, not far from us."

"Ay, we'll be practically neighbors all summer," said Brian, "only Craig and his Uncle Angus live here. Angus has been the castle caretaker for most of his life."

"And I'm just out here for the summer to help him," added Craig. "It's a nice break and besides, there's a lot to do this year, since Mr. Beattie wants to start opening the castle on weekends to the public."

To Jaynie, all this matter-of-fact conversation about castles was simply incredible. She was delighted. Standing in front of this castle, she caught herself wondering if some of the thrill was caused by the sparkling gray-blue eyes of handsome Brian, who stood in front of her, and touched her so warmly with his smile.

Suddenly, she felt cautious as she realized that Tim had a charming smile, too, and that she had been just as taken with him when they had first met. And look at the pain he caused, she thought bitterly. Well, I'm not going to be such an easy mark this time, she resolved.

Just then, a tall, pale girl turned the corner of the castle and walked across the damp grass. Brian waved at her and said, "Here comes Liz."

It was the same girl Jaynie had seen at the window in the turret. She was actually quite pretty, although perhaps too thin. Her long hair, on closer inspection, was white, rather than yellow.

"Hello, are you Jaynie?" she asked in a whispery voice.

"Yes, and you must be Liz. I'm glad to finally meet you too." Jaynie smiled, trying not to reveal her curiosity about the tall, wispy girl in the tight jeans.

"I've been looking forward to meeting you all spring," Liz said. She turned to Evelyn and continued, "Since Evelyn told us you were coming over to stay with her. I *have* been wanting to meet you, yes." She emphasized the word "have" and offered Jaynie a faint smile that curled up the corners of her lips for a brief second, then disappeared—a smile that seemed strangely out of place on Liz's solemn face.

# Chapter Four

The warmth and friendliness of Jaynie's Scottish hosts made up for the weather outside and the dampness of the enormous old kitchen in the rear of the castle where the five of them sipped hot tea and ate lentil soup. The fire in the hearth was small, and didn't warm the room enough.

As they ate, Jaynie noticed that Liz acted a bit strangely, somewhat aloof and reserved, yet not unfriendly. She seemed constantly distracted and indifferent to the conversation around her. Yet she seemed sincere whenever she said that she was glad Jaynie had joined them, which she mentioned often. The boys talked enthusiastically about Fermleven, occasionally referring to some person or incident from school. Craig was obviously glad to have Evelyn around—Jaynie could see that—and Brian was charming and gracious. In spite of her resolution to be wary, she was comforted by his warmth and sensitivity, and he soon had her feeling right at home.

Near the end of lunch, Jaynie tried to draw Liz into the conversation, since she seemed to be something of a fifth wheel, with everyone else pairing off quite comfortably.

"I was looking at your photographs last night. Evelyn says you're quite serious about your photography. Do you plan to make a career of it?" she asked as Brian began to clear the table.

"No, there isn't time. Not enough time, I don't think." Liz offered that faint, out of place smile again. Jaynie asked what it was that was taking up her time, expecting her to say something about furnishing Fermleven with her brother and father.

"Oh, nothing in particular. It's just that time is short. Generally short." Her face reflected a deep longing for something that wasn't there and her eyes drifted off with some unspoken thought. Jaynie was afraid she had said something wrong.

"I was particularly taken with the one of Fiona's Rock down at Loch Ferm." Jaynie was not exactly sure why she had said that so enthusiastically. She certainly hadn't meant that she *liked* the photo. On the other hand, some force, maybe some need for politeness, made her say it, and say it with an unyielding conviction.

Liz smiled at Jaynie, longer than usual, and asked her if she would like to see it. Jaynie thought she meant a copy or even the original of the photo.

"No, Jaynie, the real Loch Ferm. Why don't we hike down to see it? Since I prepared lunch for the group, I don't have to clean up."

Jaynie was surprised at how pleasant the walk was down the hill and through the glen, to Loch Ferm. Patches of blue sky were shining through the low clouds turning them into white, fluffy ones. Even Liz became more sunny as much as she was able to, smiling, and even cracking a joke now and then. She seemed somehow different than when she was with the others, Jaynie thought.

"You know my brother has been dying to meet you, ever since he saw your picture," she said as they entered the tight little clump of pine trees that ringed the loch.

"Saw my picture? When was that?" Jaynie asked.

"Oh, Evelyn has been talking about you ever since she returned from America at the end of the semester, showing all her friends pictures she took of people in Cincinnati, your high school—talking about how good your family was to her, how much she likes you. Brian's been anxious to meet you ever since Evelyn started writing letters about you to Craig last fall. I think he's in love with you

31

just from Evie's letters. He's been badgering her for details about you and Tim, too. He's afraid you two will get back together."

"Well, I'm not so sure that I'm ready for him or anyone else to take Tim's place," Jaynie snapped. She was immediately sorry. After all, it wasn't Liz's fault. "I'm sorry, Liz," she said. "It's just that I'm kind of mad at all men right now." Liz didn't say anything so Jaynie tried to change the subject. "Evelyn's told me a lot about you, you know. It sounds like you two have been friends for a long time."

The air beneath the trees was cool, the scattered sunlight blocked out by the thick foliage. "Evelyn—" Liz paused a moment, considering, then continued. "She thinks of you as her best friend *now*." The way she stressed "now" worried Jaynie. There was a time, of course, when Evelyn's best friend would have been Liz. Jaynie felt sorry for her.

"Here's the loch. Come meet it."

*Meet* it? thought Jaynie.

As they walked down the long green swath of grass to the rocky edge of the water, Jaynie's face lit up with astonishment. Could this lovely spot be the same place she saw in the weird photograph over her bed? The blue water sparkled in the sunlight; the green grass that led from it up to the trees looked and felt like a soft mossy carpet, just waiting for picnics. How could Liz have made this romantic setting look like something so ghostly, so threatening and uninviting? Was it just the character of the day she took the photo? Or had she used some trick photography to create that eerie effect?

"Wow! It's lovely!" Jaynie said. "Is that Fiona's Rock over there?" She pointed to a large rock about thirty feet high, that rose up out of the water, stark and fortress-like. The grayish-purple moss that covered it contrasted with the glittering green and blue that surrounded it.

"Ay, that's it. Walk over with me. I want to show you something I think *you* will find most interesting. Come quickly, it's late."

They walked quickly toward Fiona's Rock. When they got there, Liz climbed up to the top and turned to Jaynie. "Here, take my hand," she offered. She grabbed Jaynie's hand firmly and hoisted her up with one extraordinary pull. Then, Jaynie found herself looking at one of the most breathtaking views she had ever seen. Liz pointed across the trees they had just passed through and up the dark green lawn toward Fermleven Manor. There, glimmering against the blue sky, was the gray wall of the castle, now looking silvery in the sunshine. All it needed were flags waving from the pointed roofs of the turrets and Jaynie could have believed she was back in Camelot. She looked at Liz and gave her a broad smile, hoping Liz understood how thrilled she was to be there. As if Liz could read her thoughts, she said, "We're really glad you're here, Jaynie. I've

33

been wanting to meet you as much as Brian has. In some ways, even more, I think."

"Really? Why?" This didn't seem like the depressed and moody girl that Evelyn had warned her of the night before.

"Oh, I'm not sure. Just a feeling. A hunch, but a strong one, that you and I may have a lot in common." Liz looked at Jaynie long and hard, and that faint corner-of-the-mouth smile appeared again, then quickly vanished. Changing the subject, she grabbed Jaynie's hand and pulled her out to the middle of the rock, closer to the edge above the glass-like water below. "See this red mark?"

Jaynie looked down, and there in the thick purple moss that covered the top of the rock was a clear spot where the gray stone shone through. In the middle of the clear area was a deep blood-red spot that looked as if the color penetrated far down into the very granite itself.

"What is it?" asked Jaynie, intrigued by its uniqueness. Nowhere else on the rock, as far as Jaynie could see, were there any other discolorations or strange markings.

"Fiona's last kiss," answered Liz solemnly. She spoke reverently, in the hushed tone of someone standing in the back of a cathedral. "The kiss of blood!"

"What do you mean? I don't follow you," said Jaynie, a bit nervous at Liz's sudden seriousness, wondering why this red spot should evoke such solemnity.

"Lady Fiona, a princess from the Highlands, died here many centuries ago."

"Yes, I know, Evelyn told me last night when we were looking at your photograph, that there had been a suicide here."

Liz repeated what she had just said, "Fiona was a Highland princess. She died here, Jaynie." She said it as if it should have some greater importance than it seemed to Jaynie, an importance that Liz would eventually reveal to her.

"But why is this spot red? Is it really the lip-print of a kiss?"

Liz continued her story, reciting it mechanically, sounding like a schoolgirl with a lesson she had memorized and repeated to herself, or to others, many, many times.

"When Fiona found the body of her slain lover, she kissed his wound and with bloody lips, ran to this great rock. She threw herself down upon it at this very spot, and kissed it, leaving the lip-print that you see there. Her tears sealed the blood into the stone for eternity. Then she threw herself into the loch and was never seen again."

She put her thin arm around Jaynie's waist and walked her over to the craggy edge of the rock, and with a firm pressure on her hips, pushed Jaynie down on her knees. Liz knelt, too and then bent forward, clutching the edge with both hands, and leaning far out over the water, stared down into its depths. Jaynie leaned over and stared down, wondering what Liz was looking for so intently. All Jaynie could see was the water, tinged blue by the sky, deep, motionless, and tranquil.

Without warning, in the same monotone, Liz added, "And they found only her slippers and a scarf. Craig's Uncle Angus says she will return someday—and when she does, it will be for revenge!

Jaynie trembled, and asked, "Revenge? Against what? Against whom?"

Liz pulled her back, spun her around, and knelt before her. She clutched Jaynie's shoulders tightly with both hands and looked her in the eye. "You must read *Macbeth!*"

She returned to her blank stare over the ledge, cutting off further discussion. Jaynie looked back into the water too and saw their reflections leap out from the edge of the cliff. *Macbeth*? she wondered. Jaynie saw Liz's reflection mirrored next to her own, riffled there on the moving water, as if the two girls were floating on the surface, or in the sky.

Their heads seemed to bob back and forth, closer together and then separating, Liz's on the right, and her own on the left, together, apart, together, apart. Or *was* that her own reflection? It had to be, and yet it didn't look exactly right, wiggled out of shape by the ripples. Of course it was! She was on the left, Liz was on the right, and — and the one in — She blinked and shook her head.

The face in the middle!! Between them!!

Jaynie shut her eyes tightly and opened them as wide as she could. Yes, there was a *third* face! In between them! And its cold eyes never blinked— it was the stare of the dead!

# Chapter Five

Jaynie was glad to get back to the castle. She said nothing to Liz about the corpse-like face she thought she had seen. In fact, she tried to put the image out of her mind, telling herself it was just some kind of optical illusion.

"You'll never see the whole castle in one afternoon," remarked Brian, when the two girls returned. "Let's just go through some of the larger rooms. We'll have to see the rest of them another day." He looked at Jaynie, and asked hopefully, "You *will* be here all summer, won't you?"

Jaynie gave him a quick nod of her head. She told him she thought it would be fabulous to come back often, and really get to know the castle.

"Great," Brian answered enthusiastically. "We

can use your help with the Scottish Historical Association's gala affair in August. Would you like to be a scullery maid or a hostess?" he kidded.

"I think I'd prefer to be the hostess. I would rather be a lady than a peasant girl," Jaynie said jokingly. They all laughed, and she could see herself helping to prepare Fermleven Manor for the burst of festivities. She tried to picture modern Scots in an ancient setting that must have witnessed thousands of such extravaganzas in more medieval, more savage times.

The five of them trekked off down a hall, chatting about the most recent renovations, and paying particular attention to the areas that needed no modern touch-ups, the places still basking in the authentic glow of the past. Brian proudly led the way and his courteous manner made Jaynie think that in an earlier age, he could have actually been the lord—or "laird" as she was soon to learn—of Fermleven Manor. Occasionally he put his arm lightly around her shoulders as he ushered her through a narrow doorway. She liked that. Grabbing each other's hand now and then, Evelyn and Craig kept rather close to each other and shared a private laugh every so often. It gave her a good feeling to see the two of them together. Occasionally, a memory of her and Tim flashed across her mind and she felt a pang of loneliness. But she was happy for Evelyn. Liz stayed to herself, Jaynie noticed, looking rather bored. She wondered if Liz had a boyfriend, then she remembered what she had said earlier about having a lot in common with Jaynie. She realized now that Liz was probably referring to some boy who had hurt her, too. Why else would she make such an effort to take Jaynie to Fiona's Rock and tell her the story behind it? Liz certainly had seemed to be carried away by the idea of Fiona returning for revenge. Although she had only known this girl for a few hours, Jaynie suddenly felt that they knew each other in a way that Evelyn could never understand.

"I think it's about time to go, unfortunately," announced Craig, as the afternoon began to draw to a close. "Time sure flies."

"And I still haven't met your Uncle Angus, yet," reminded Jaynie, disappointedly.

"Well, he drove into the village today to go shopping, and I guess something's delayed him. Sometimes he loses track of the hours, like he steps into a time-warp—and when he emerges, it's much later than he expected. Eccentricity, I suppose. Looks like you'll just have to wait till next time to meet him. Don't worry, he'll last. He's indestructible."

"But now we better get going, so we won't hit the rush hour in Edinburgh," said Brian. He looked at Jaynie directly and smiled broadly. "Say, why don't you drive back with me? Liz can go with Evelyn. I'd like to show you some scenic places on the back road."

Jaynie looked over at Evelyn who made up her mind for her friend with a quick nod. "Liz and I haven't had a good chance to talk since I got back.

You go on." Jaynie could tell that Evelyn's eagerness was not over a private talk with Liz, but rather to let her have some time alone with Brian. Jaynie had to admit to herself that she was thrilled. She decided she definitely wanted to get to know this boy who talked of castles and politics as familiarly as if he were talking about school and sports. But she wasn't ready to think of him in a romantic way. She couldn't let herself do that—the risk of getting hurt was too great.

They all said goodbye to Craig, and got in their cars and left. Jaynie looked back over the seat and out the rear window at the castle as Brian drove down the rocky drive.

"I can imagine what a job it must have been to restore the place," she said.

"Actually, an awful lot was done by Uncle Angus. Everyone calls him 'uncle,' so don't be afraid to call him that when you meet him. I guess he knows every nook and cranny better than anyone. You'll like him. Oh, he's mysterious in some ways. Eccentric. A magician, too. He knows a lot of old legends and folk tales about Scotland, especially this area in Fife." Brian paused for a moment. "Oh, there are all sorts of places you should see while you're here this summer, Jaynie. I could show you romantic little spots that I know like the back of my hand."

"Well," Jaynie said, her caution overtaking her again. "Well, if you have any free time, I'd like to have you show me around." She almost wished she hadn't said it. She knew it would be a while before she could trust her feelings again, and, after all, she had only just met Brian. She didn't want to be misled by his good looks and Scottish charm. She knew that a twinkling eye and quick handsome smile, even one that touched her so deeply, might lead nowhere. Or might lead to another painful separation and disappointment. Again, she thought of Tim. And California. For a second or two, the faint tremor of anger rumbled in her, and she didn't hear what Brian was saying.

"What?" she asked. "I didn't hear you. I was watching the traffic. I'm just not used to people driving on the left side of the road. It makes me jumpy, because we drive on the right in the States."

"How peculiar!" he teased. "And do you have a lot of accidents driving that way?"

Jaynie laughed. "Well, as a matter of fact, we do." It was apparent that they were enjoying each other's company. In spite of her hesitation, Jaynie was letting herself have fun. It wasn't hard. Brian was thoroughly charming.

"Would you like to try driving on the 'wrong' side of the road?" he offered. "It's not very hard. You'll probably feel awkward at first, but you'll get over it. You really should learn since you may have to drive while you're here." He pulled over onto the shoulder of the road by a rough log fence. There was a broad green glen with some horses quietly chomping on grass and flicking their tails over their rumps in idle contentment.

"Slide over, lass." He got in and gave her

a friendly pat on her thigh. Jaynie slid behind the wheel.

"I guess I'll just pretend I'm driving on a one-way street for awhile, until I get my bearings," she said.

The car was a Porsche. She had never driven such an expensive or powerful car before. As she looked over her right shoulder to see if any traffic was coming, her eyes caught Brian's and he smiled encouragingly. "You can do it," he assured her.

She edged the car out onto the narrow two-lane asphalt road that bent and wound its way through farmland and gently rolling hills. They drove down a steep hill and onto a long straight stretch of highway, her hands sweaty and clutching the steering wheel more tightly than usual. She noticed two cars coming along, and surprised herself by watching them closely to see if they would stay on their side of the road. How foolish! she thought, as they whizzed past her. *They* know what side to drive on; it's me who has to watch out.

"What do you think?" asked Brian, who had his arm over the back seat, reassuringly, his hand touching Jaynie's long hair where it fell onto her shoulders. "Does it seem funny to you?"

"Uh, yes," she admitted, afraid to take her eyes off the road.

"Make a right turn up here on the other side of this cottage." He slipped his hand up under her hair and squeezed the back of her neck affectionately.

His hand felt good on her neck, but Jaynie

worried about the bridge coming up, and forgot she was driving on the left side of the road. She angled the Porsche into the right lane to make the right-hand turn. As she slowed down, Brian tapped her shoulder and said, "Don't forget where you are, lass. A right turn is still from the left lane here."

"Of course." Jaynie blushed, feeling foolish, and looked over her left shoulder to make sure the coast was clear before she swung back into the other lane. But while her head was still turned, Brian grabbed her neck again, this time harder.

"Jaynie, get over! Quick! There's a car coming! Get over!"

Jaynie's head swivelled around like a puppet's. She looked ahead, down the road. A small red car had just leapt into view around a bend, coming straight at them, fast. There wouldn't be time for the red car to swerve.

"Jaynie!" Brian shouted.

A queasy pinching in her stomach made her think something inside of her had collapsed. Her hands froze on the steering wheel. They wouldn't respond. Her mouth went dry, as she realized she had lost control. Of the car—and herself.

And then a thin, high-pitched voice sounded in her head.

*Speed up, step on it, or you'll miss your chance.*

Jaynie closed her eyes. Chance for what? Chance for what? It's almost on us — it's — Her mind went blank.

The next thing she knew the car was spinning furiously out of control, sliding away from the sickening crunch that filled her ears, pitching her over onto Brian's lap, as the car toppled into a steep ravine on the side of the road. Brian jolted forward, cried out in pain, and flopped back against the seat, his head thrown back on the head rest limply. An ugly gash stretched across his forehead.

Terrified, Jaynie grabbed his head in her hands and watched the blood trickle down toward his left eye. Have I killed him? she thought, horrified, turning his pale face toward her. She shouted his name and pulled him closer. "Brian! Brian! I'm sorry!" Her own head was swimming and she felt nauseous. "I'll make it well, I will!"

Hysterically, she leaned toward him, and pressed her lips on his forehead. She licked a drop of blood that was about to run onto his closed eyelid. She continued licking it, running her tongue through his bloodsoaked eyebrow. She sucked on the cut and swallowed the blood. "Please, Brian!" She kissed him, on his cut, tasting the warm red life flowing from him, hoping that somehow all the blood would go away, and the wound would heal. She kissed him again, this time on the lips, and then slumped unconsciously with her arms still around him.

When the driver from the red car reached them and managed to open the door, he found a young boy passed out in the arms of a pretty girl, both bleeding, he thought, until he wiped the blood from the girl's lips.

David Macdonald hung up the phone and returned to the guest room.

"Brian got off with just a few stitches in his forehead. No concussion or anything serious. It's a miracle that you two are all right."

Jaynie sat up in bed, her stomach jittery and the bump on her own head throbbing furiously. She thought there must be some sadistic demon inside her skull, hammering to get out. She still felt dizzy, and couldn't remember anything between the time she had spotted the red car, and when she had woken up in the Macdonald's guest room, apparently several hours later.

"You look absolutely exhausted," Mrs. Macdonald said. What you really need is a solid night's rest." Jaynie agreed, and as the family trudged downstairs for dinner, she heard Mrs. Macdonald utter something about jetlag.

What a way to begin a visit with people I hardly even know, she told herself. What must they think! Listlessly, she drifted off to sleep where, in the refuge of unconsciousness, she would not have to think about herself, Brian, the car or the blame.

A little after midnight, she awoke.

It was dark. She was clutching her pillow tightly in both arms.

Then she heard it.

"Jaaay-nieee!"

Her head still ached from the car wreck. The dream-voice seemed to be howling painfully inside her skull. The second call came even louder, stronger, and reverberated behind her forehead for what felt like an achingly long time. There was a struggling tone in the voice that mingled with her own suffering. She sat up erect and rubbed her eyes, trying to wipe away a feeling of dizziness.

The photo of Loch Ferm was brilliant with an electrifying glow that throbbed and pulsated between purple and green, green and purple, a continuously expanding and contracting aura of color and light. Jaynie felt her head throb from the spot where a large lump had formed. She wanted to lie back down and press her head as hard as she could into her pillow to dull the pain, but then she noticed the figure of Fiona, wrapped in fronds and reeds, standing with her arms slightly raised, palms upward as in supplication.

Jaynie got up as she had the night before and placed her palms against either side of the picture to steady herself and lean closely into it. This time she vaguely knew what to expect. When she put her lips within an inch of the glass and breathed upon it, the figure of the young girl opened her mouth grotesquely and in the array of bubbles that rose to the water's surface, the message of the night before was repeated, this time more clearly. And more desperately—a cry of pain and anguish.

"All that could be found!!"

Jaynie listened closely, her eyes shut tightly, letting the desperation in the words penetrate her consciousness, taking it inside her, making it her own.

Then the agonizing tone of the spirit stabbed through her brain, to the very core of her own memories, and she sensed and felt the dark, profound pain of sorrow and loss.

Reopening her eyes, she watched the greenish light fade as the figure of Fiona moved back into darkness and immobility.

Too soon! Jaynie thought. Don't leave so soon. I hurt, too.

Then she spoke, softly, tenderly, to the receding figure, "Whoever you are, whatever you are— I think I know you!"

# Chapter Six

"Brian fancies you, you know. I knew he would. He couldn't wait to meet you."

Evelyn had watched it start to blossom in the two days since the accident. "And believe me, Jaynie, Brian doesn't hold you responsible for the accident."

Jaynie smiled half-heartedly. "I wish I could believe that, but it just seems so—oh, I don't know—it doesn't seem right—so soon." Jaynie frowned.

"Look, the accident wasn't really your fault. The other driver admitted he was speeding, and—listen, even Scottish drivers often pull over onto the right side to make a right turn on those little back roads. It was *not* your fault, now get that through your head."

"But, Evelyn, something happened to me at the last moment, before that red car swiped us. I know I panicked and lost control, but something inside me—inside my head, I guess—*wanted* me to lose control. I know I'm not suicidal or anything, but I had the strangest sensation that, in the split second before we crashed, I had a chance to—end it—do something wrong or commit some evil and violent act. I *wanted* to. Don't you see? I just thought to myself: here's your chance, don't miss your chance. And past that, my mind just blanks."

"But, Jaynie!" After two days of similar arguments, Evelyn was getting exasperated with her friend's stubbornness. "People are not responsible for their actions, or their thoughts in moments of panic. That's what panic is—a real loss of control. You can't make yourself do what you know you should. In fact, when you panic, you might not even *know* what you should do.

"Try to forget what happened and forgive yourself. Look at the bright side. The accident gave you and Brian a great opportunity to get to know each other. The two of you have covered more ground in the last couple of days than you would have in weeks. It would be great if you two really hit it off. Listen, Jaynie, he's kind, intelligent, not to mention wealthy, and, to use another Scottish expression," Evelyn winked at Jaynie, "—he's dishy." She said it sensuously, romantically.

50

"Well, I thought Tim was all of those things, too, and look where that got me," Jaynie grumbled. She realized that Evelyn meant well, but she was beginning to get annoyed with the fact that her friend was determined to push Jaynie into a relationship with Brian. No matter how nice Brian was, Jaynie could not be convinced that going out with him would just automatically erase all of the hurt Tim had caused her. And besides, how did she know that Brian wouldn't end up treating her the same way? She pointed that out to Evelyn.

"Oh, I don't think Brian would act that way," her friend answered quickly. "I've known him a long time, Jaynie, and I've never seen him mistreat any of the girls he's gone out with."

Jaynie couldn't easily argue with that, so she let the subject drop. But she was still unconvinced. After all, she told herself, she would only be in Scotland for the summer, and that would be a perfect excuse for Brian to break up with her. Still . . . as Evelyn had said, he was "dishy" and maybe it wouldn't hurt to just be friends with him. She forced herself to cheer up and turned to Evelyn. "Did you say dishy? That sounds like one of our expressions. We say that someone's a real dish." Jaynie chuckled to herself. Dishy! Brian certainly was that!

After dinner that evening, the Macdonalds invited the girls to play cards, but Jaynie excused herself, saying she wanted to go to bed early. Mrs. Macdonald approved heartily.

"Are you sleeping properly?" she asked.

"Oh, yes ma'am. Like a rock. The past two nights I slept so soundly that when I woke up, I fell right back to sleep," she said.

David Macdonald looked up from his newspaper, puzzled. "It would seem to me that if you're waking up in the night, then you mustn't be sleeping very soundly."

"Well, what wakes me, Mr. Mac, are my dreams. But ever since the accident, they've been pleasant dreams, and I fall right back to sleep."

Evelyn asked, "What are your dreams about? I remember when we formed the dream club at school last year, your dreams seemed to be particularly powerful."

"Oh, that's true, especially the deep ones," Jaynie recalled. "Last night and the night before, when I woke up from one, I just had this really strong sensation that I've been getting to know someone."

"Well, that makes sense. Your dream life is confirming your waking life, just like Miss Kurzberg told us last year. You've been getting to know Brian over the last few days."

"Ay, and David and me," chimed in Betty Macdonald with a motherly smile.

"That's true," agreed Jaynie. But you don't know about all my other dreams, she thought. Ever since the accident, Jaynie had had a recurring dream about Tim that always ended up with him walking away from her, arm in arm with his California girlfriend. These dreams had occurred so often that Jaynie was getting used to them. In the beginning, when she first started having them, she would wake up crying, with the image of Tim and that other girl still fresh in her mind. As time went on, though, that hurt had turned into anger and Jaynie would wake up with a fury in her heart.

She said goodnight and went upstairs, reflecting on what had just been said. She felt uncomfortably wrong about it. True, she was getting to know the Macdonalds and Brian and his father and mother and Liz. But that's not what my dreams are about, she thought to herself as she pulled down the blankets and drew the curtains on the window. That would be a shallow dream, and I know what I'm having are deep, psychic dreams, the kind that Miss Kurzberg says come from your deep subconscious. She paused at the window, staring out at the immense gray hump of Ronan's Hill across the road. It's more like that hill, she thought, something deep in the earth, some secret buried so far down that no one knows its meaning yet. It's some destiny not yet revealed, some person maybe, some new identity glimpsed piece by piece each night, slowly coming together in sleep to make a whole. A secret buried deep, deep. But buried where?

Buried, not in the earth or rock of a hill, but deep down, far down inside—of—perhaps me. Perhaps it is me who I'm getting to know in my dreams. Miss Kurzberg's theory was that our dreams are always about ourselves, Jaynie told herself as she crawled into bed and pulled her security pillow up to her chin.

\* \* \*

The following day Jaynie enjoyed herself enough to get over the moody slump she had fallen into since the car wreck. It helped her feel accepted, and forgiven, when Ian Beattie kept referring to the project as "Jaynie's grand idea." The third day Jaynie was visiting Brian in Tweedkeith, while he was still in bed, she remarked that Fermleven would be perfect for postcards or travel brochures on Scotland. Ian Beattie seized upon the idea and decided that on the next "bonnie day" they should all return to Fermleven and let Liz take some photographs that could be used to put together a brochure on Fermleven Manor itself.

The day was perfect for hunting out the most dramatic vistas around the estate. Everyone had such a good time, they even decided to spend the night, get up early in the morning, if the day proved clear, and get a shot of the sun rising over Loch Ferm. Jaynie was exuberant as she realized that the car wreck was a thing of the past, and that everyone was treating her like one of the family.

In the evening, Uncle Angus cooked a lamb stew, and the merry gathering ate and drank beer around a large crackling fire. Angus was a crafty little man of a thousand wrinkles and twitches. His shaggy white hair fell in tangles to his shoulders, his beak nose protruded, and his eyes gleamed with an other-worldly fire.

As the beer worked its sleepy effect of breaking down disbelief, the "young 'uns," as Uncle Angus called them, fell into that state of gullibility that a fireplace, a late hour, and a good story teller could so easily produce in fertile imaginations. Late into the night, they sat and listened to Uncle Angus tell stories.

Jaynie found these tales truly delightful, until he told his third story. Suddenly, as Angus was speaking, Jaynie imagined the youthful quality behind his tough wrinkles to be perhaps a deliberate attempt on his part to conceal something sinister. He seemed to look directly at her as he began the story.

"Once there was a visitor to the Highlands, a young girl not unlike yourself," he spat at Jaynie with a dramatic flourish of his finger, pointing at her startled face.

"She had come to disturb the grave of a Highland lad who had been a brave warrior and was killed treacherously in a clan feud. It seemed, now, that the young girl, who happened to be from America, thought she was the slain warrior's twin sister who had been reincarnated. She wanted to dig the body up to see if there was any resemblance. Well, she dug it up, mind you, and do you know what she discovered?" He looked directly at Jaynie, menacingly.

"No."

"She saw a skeleton."

"And did it look like her?" asked Craig.

"Ay, her own face turned into a hideous bone-white skull."

Later, Jaynie asked Craig why Angus seemed to have turned on her.

"Well," Craig said, "nobody ever knows exactly what's brewing in that old man's head, but I wouldn't worry about it too much."

They said goodnight and Craig went into the room that he and Brian were sharing for the night. Brian had gone to bed early since Doctor Campbell ordered him to take it easy and get plenty of rest. When he said he would see everyone in the morning, she had the distinct feeling that he was looking only at her.

Jaynie walked down the long, dimly lit corridor to the bedroom she was using. The room was decorated in a medieval style, with a coat of arms on the wall, a luxurious tapestry hanging behind the big wide bed, and a display of swords and daggers on another wall.

When she reached her door, a faint footstep behind her made her jump.

"Liz!" she gulped in relief. "Oh, you scared me! I thought maybe Evelyn had gotten up, but no one answered."

Liz motioned to Jaynie to step over toward her room. She stood there solemnly like a priestess attending a ceremony of great importance. From behind her snow white hair, which fell forward over her face, came a voice—that faint, breathless whisper that sounded as if she were speaking from a vacuum located a long distance away.

"Jaynie, you must not be deceived by the merriment of the day. Do not allow it to lead you into a false gladness."

What could Liz be talking about in such oddly

stilted language? Jaynie wondered. What did she mean by "merriment" and "false gladness?" The phrasing sounded archaic and just a bit too creepy for Jaynie. She was about to say goodnight when the vague, distracted voice continued.

"The photographs we took today must be altered. They must render this a place of tragedy, for so it is! They must reveal the unleashing of fiends and attest to the murder in cold blood. Remember, Jaynie, the blood on the rock, the blood on my brother, the blood on your own lips! Remember that blood is never, never warm!"

Jaynie couldn't take it any longer, this was too creepy. As much as she wanted to get to know Liz, she was just too tired to comprehend what she was saying right now. She felt it was important, though, and decided to ask Liz about it first thing in the morning. "Listen," she said, "I'm really too tired to talk about this tonight, but I want to hear all about it tomorrow, okay? Goodnight."

Liz didn't answer Jaynie, but silently turned to go back to her own room. Jaynie stood at the door until she heard the door to Liz's room shut and as it did, she suddenly felt a cold tingling sensation run down her arms.

# Chapter Seven

When she awoke, the grandfather clock down below in the grand foyer was striking an eerie midnight. She got up and put on her robe, then wandered aimlessly over to the window, opened it, and saw a crescent moon shining brightly overhead.

How beautiful and peaceful it looks! she thought.

Tonight would be perfect for star watching, out in the country, miles from any city lights, and from the wall of a castle!

She remembered that a tower ran up the side of the wall alongside her window. It would not be difficult to find the tower room, she assured herself. She would just have to climb the stairs outside her door. It would be dark, but she could feel her way up them and once on the castle wall, she'd have the moonlight.

She stepped out into the hallway, barely able to see anything. The small lamp down the hall near Evelyn's room was out. It doesn't matter, she thought, I know where I'm going. She found the tower stairs and began the long twisting climb to the top.

The cold flat stones chilled her bare feet. She wouldn't stay out long, just a couple of minutes to see Fermleven Manor drenched in pale moonlight. She imagined what it would be like under a full moon, hoping the heavy cloudcover would be gone then. She wanted to see this fairyland clothed in the complete raiment of moonlight and magic. She walked up the cold steps, where centuries of footsteps had worn them down, the footsteps of men and women, children, knights and warriors, now dead and buried throughout Britain, individuals who were the ghostly pieces of Scottish history and myth. She thought about those legends—round and round they went in her head—dragons, witches, wizards, sorcerers, magic swords, poisoned drinks, cups of blood, tombs, the dead, the undead—stop!!

She halted on the stair. "Wait a minute," she gasped. "I'm losing my breath! My head is spinning too fast!"

She finished her climb, and felt along the wall for the door. The handle creaked in its rusty moorings as she turned it, and she pushed hard against the wooden door with her shoulder but it wouldn't give. She tried again, and slowly, with loud, echoing creaks and groans from the hinges, the heavy door inched open, and again she was standing under the clear night sky.

What a view! she thought, standing there, breathless, in the crisp night air. She felt dizzy and drunk and bewitched. How lucky I am to be here and see all this! How romantic it would be if Tim could— No!

She couldn't understand why that thought kept occurring to her. She did *not,* she told herself, want him to be up here. She had hoped to put him completely out of her thoughts. There were just too many other things to think about. She was angry with herself for spoiling the night and the view. It seemed that every time she started feeling good, something inside would remind her of Tim, and that other girl, and she became consumed by anger and the desire to get even. She really didn't want to think of him right now— or anymore. Maybe Brian could help her forget the pain she felt, after all.

She was about to turn and go back to the tower, when she heard someone call to her from far down below.

She leaned over the parapet and looked at the gravel drive but saw no one. Then she heard it again.

"Jaaay-nieee!"

A young girl's voice, calling from far away.

She looked down. Of course, she thought to

herself, just because I can't see anyone down there doesn't mean anything. Someone might be hiding in the shadows of the building, or concealed down in the trees, or maybe even— She had a hunch. As she held her breath, waiting for the call to be repeated, she fixed her gaze on Loch Ferm, shimmering darkly in the pale moonlight. She heard her name called yet another time. Now she was sure the caller was down at the loch.

Somehow it sounded familiar to her, but she wasn't sure why. What terrified her was the pitifully helpless tone in the voice, the pleading quality that carried a desperate cry for help.

Jaynie had the uncanny sensation that she had experienced all of this before. She wished the voice would call again; she wanted to recognize it, find out who it was. She wanted to see everything she could down at the loch, for she sensed that something horrible was going on down there, something that might be happening to her if she were down there. And *that* thought horrified her.

Then, without warning, there appeared a pool of light in the water at the base of the rock. It began to glow and grow brighter. Jaynie looked harder. It did grow brighter! Turning into an unearthly seagreen, flooding up to the surface, splashing a tint on the lower part of the rock, a hidden source of illumination was quietly and inexorably at work. It created a greenish floodlight that seemed to come from the very depths of the earth itself with an intensity so bright that she could make out the finest features of the scene—a scene lit up especially for Jaynie's viewing.

In a flash of realization, she gasped and pushed her palms against her temple. She knew what would happen next! Like watching an old movie that was being re-run on television for the fourth or fifth time, she knew what would happen!

No, no! she thought. I don't want to see it! I don't want to see it!

But then—a slender wraithlike figure appeared, glimmering in a white gown, hair twisted with vines and loch moss and dripping with the slime of rotting algae. Gracefully, as in a ballet, it ascended out of the water, taking small delicate steps up the shore to the bank of the rock. For a brief moment the spectral image disappeared behind it, and then slowly reappeared on the top of the rock.

Jaynie felt dizzy. But the creature had come from the depths of the loch. And then it dawned on Jaynie . . .

"Fiona!" she whispered. "She's returned to the rock!"

And with the precision of a ceremony repeated night after night, the ghostly shape of the dead princess walked to the bloody lip-print, knelt by it reverently and pressed her wet mouth against the dark red stain. While she held that position for a few seconds, the whole landscape seemed to be hushed. Everything—trees, birds, hills, sheep, rocks, moors—all of nature seemed to be looking the other way, except Jaynie, the sole, reluctant witness, paralyzed with terror.

Then the figure rose and without turning its head to either side, walked straight to the edge of the rock—and jumped! As the body hit the water, the green light that created the aura around the rock lit up in a blinding flash, and then vanished, as quickly and silently as Fiona. Then the water closed over her body as the normal hue of moonlight closed over the great flat rock.

No! No! Jaynie tried to shout it, but no sound left her throat, except for a fierce gasping for air. Why *me!* She placed her hands over her eyes and turned her back to the scene for several minutes, thinking, thinking, wondering why all this seemed so familiar to her. Then she lunged around and looked down toward the loch one last time. All she could see was the moonlight breaking apart on the ripples of the water. All at once, she was painfully aware of how cold her feet were, as if the stones in the wall were maliciously forcing icy needles into them.

"No," she screamed, as she ran back to the tower door.

# Chapter Eight

When Jaynie heard the shattering crash of thunder, she was afraid to open her eyes. She vaguely sensed that she had not slept well and had no idea of the time. As she was struggling to sort out the confusing memories of the night, another clap of thunder rattled the glass in the window, and she knew that they would not be photographing today.

After getting dressed, Jaynie went downstairs to the stone kitchen. The room was filled with the aroma of eggs, bacon, and porridge. When Jaynie arrived, everyone was clustered around the fire drinking tea and keeping warm, everyone except Ian Beattie and Liz. Uncle Angus was at the stove poking a long crooked fork at strips of bacon in a heavy iron skillet.

"Good morning, Jaynie," piped up Craig. "Welcome to Thunder Castle! The storm isn't as bad as it sounds from inside here. These walls amplify every crack of thunder and downpour of rain. There's a lot in here to rattle and echo. But, not to worry. In five hundred years, no storm has yet swept Fermleven away."

Brian got up to pour Jaynie some coffee. "None are likely to destroy the place this summer."

"How thoughtful!" she said. "You remembered my morning coffee. I'm a wreck without it."

"Ay," he smiled. "But we may make a morning tea drinker out of you before you leave."

"How's your head?" she asked. "Is it feeling better?"

"Sure is. I'm sure Doctor Campbell will be taking the stitches out soon." He shrugged, indicating there was nothing to it.

"Where's your father this morning?"

"Oh, he's already left for Tweedkeith. He only stayed to get the sunrise, and when he saw the rain, he decided it would last all day. Besides, I think he's got some political meeting in town this afternoon."

"All right, young 'uns, let breakfast begin," said Uncle Angus. He held the steaming platter of eggs out in front of him as the others gathered around the wooden table. "But first, I want to confirm a suspicion before it gets too late."

He stepped up behind Jaynie's chair and placed both his hands on her head, letting his gnarled,

65

arthritic fingers work their way through her hair, down to her scalp. She thought he must be feeling for lumps. She had heard that you can read someone's future by the bumps on a person's head.

"Nope! I think not," Angus said, moving over to Evelyn and repeating the strange probing.

"Again! I think not," he announced.

Craig tried to interrupt. "Uncle Angus, what are you up to?" But Uncle Angus ignored him and stepped up behind Brian.

"Be careful," said Jaynie. "Brian's head still has a tender spot."

"I'll not disturb his wound. It isn't pain I'm after, it's truth!" he answered petulantly, and began to let the tips of his fingers walk over Brian's thick curly hair. "I think not again!" He went over to Craig. "You're last, nephew."

When he had finished, Craig asked, "Okay, Uncle Angus, have you hexed us all? What should we expect? Warts? Blindness? Or will our hair just fall out?"

"I have my suspicions, lad, that's all," he answered mysteriously. He went back to the stove and began to clatter the pots and pans. He seemed frustrated, slightly angry at something. After a minute, he returned to the table.

"All right now, I'll be asking you straight-forward, and looking you each right smart in the eye. You won't fool me, not *me!*" He squinted devilishly at each of them in turn. "None of your hair is matted, and none of you have dried algae anywhere on your scalp, but one of you young 'uns—" He shook his finger at them. "Or *some* of you young 'uns were skinny dipping in the loch last night. Don't deny it! I heard it!" With that, he pointed his finger up to the ceiling, as if to call a lightning bolt down on the guilty party. Immediately, a loud clap of thunder rumbled over the countryside. The four "young 'uns" froze, watching Uncle Angus turn from an amiable breakfast chef into some stark and mean-spirited avenger. Craig broke the silence. Being used to his uncle's dramatics, he could see through a lot of wizardish bluster.

"Uncle Angus, I don't think any of us went skinny dipping last night." He turned, looking for support from each of the others, waiting for them to nod or agree with him. "You see?" Craig went on, "none of us even went outside after we turned in last night."

Jaynie gulped at that last comment and thought she better say something about her midnight stroll on the parapet, but she didn't want to weaken Craig's case. Besides, not knowing Uncle Angus as well as the others did, she was a bit jittery about getting him angry, even though she did think that he was overdoing it to be dramatic.

"You wouldna be lying to me, now would you?"

All of them shook their heads, including Jaynie.

"Well, I heard the splashing of water, and I saw your torches! Now who could it have been? Tell me! Are you going to suggest midnight prowlers?" The intonation in his voice clearly implied they would be crazy to give him such an answer. He *knew* it was one of them, and he would not be shaken in his belief. Brian broke the silence this time.

"Maybe it was Liz, Uncle Angus. Wait till she gets up and we'll ask her. But I'm sure she didn't go swimming. Maybe she went down to get some night pictures of the loch. There was bonnie little moon last night, and you know how she likes to photograph Fiona's Rock, especially under different kinds of lighting. Wait'll she comes down before you—" He looked over at Craig, who wasn't as intimidated as the rest.

"Before you hex us," Craig concluded for Brian.

The effect was perfect. They all burst into laughter, and continued to plead their innocence with the old man.

"Well, all I can say," he began, unconvinced by their claims of innocence, "is that something mighty peculiar was going on down there last night. Mighty peculiar indeed."

Jaynie knew what she wanted to ask, but was terrified to voice it. The others were chatting about how, even though the chilly night air was certainly not inviting, they would have had fun if they *had* gone skinny dipping. They continued to boast about how maybe they should go for a night swim sometime, and how they would deceive the old man. Their teasing him was all in good natured fun. But Jaynie kept quiet, weighing the possible effects of what she wanted to ask.

"Uncle Angus," she began, her voice low, and

afraid to raise her eyes from her plate and look at anyone yet. "Uncle Angus, do you think—?" She paused and glanced up at him. "I've heard that the spirit of Fiona—" She was into it now, the others had stopped talking and eating, and were listening to her. At the mention of Fiona, Uncle Angus raised his chin to look at the American girl. He squinted so hard at her that when she looked up at him, she thought he had completely shut his eyes. She rephrased the question.

"Do you think there's any truth to the legend that the Princess Fiona will return sometime? To take revenge?" There, she had said it.

There was an icy hush all around the table. Slowly, hesitantly, each of them turned to look at Uncle Angus, wondering what his reply would be. Of all the myths and legends that he enjoyed recounting, the story of the dead princess was somehow special, somehow sacred to him. He never teased about it, but took it seriously and personally. They all knew this, except Jaynie.

"Well now," Angus backed away a bit. "I won't be *forced* to talk about it. I won't! But I'll tell you this, lassie." He took another step away from her, and lowered his voice. "If—mind you, *if*—" He paused. "If she ever returns, I'm pretty sure that *I —would—recognize her.*" His speech had slowed down so much, they all feared a trance had come over him. He paused, staring intently, curiously, at Jaynie. She knew the ball was in her court, so she asked, in the firmest voice she could muster, "What does she look like, Uncle Angus?"

He spoke more softly, almost tenderly. "She was young and bonny. She didna look unlike yourself, lass!"

He uttered the last sentence in such a whisper that he was barely audible. Craig thought he detected a slight choke in his uncle's voice. Another peel of thunder broke over the castle.

"Well!" It was Brian, ready to end this uneasy, hostile mood and go on to something else. "I'll go wake Liz, and tell her to hustle, so we can start back for Tweedkeith. There won't be any picture taking today."

Craig offered to clean up the breakfast dishes and Uncle Angus, still glowering at Jaynie, backed out of the room and slunk off to do his chores. Only Jaynie and Evelyn remained seated at the table, both feeling a little uneasy.

Evelyn looked over at Jaynie and shivered with exaggeration, to let her friend know that she, too, felt uncomfortable. "C'mon, Jaynie. Let's pack our things and get out of here."

# Chapter Nine

As soon as the girls were alone, Jaynie grabbed Evelyn's arm tightly and said, "I have this feeling—something tells me . . . "

"What?"

"I think I know where Liz is!"

Stopping only to put on raincoats, they ran out into the storm.

Evelyn followed Jaynie's trail into a thick clump of trees until they emerged on the shore of the loch.

"Jaynie, what the devil are we doing out here? Liz won't be out taking pictures in *this*."

Jaynie shook her head. "She's not taking pictures. Come on!"

She began running along the pebbly shore around the loch to where Fiona's Rock sat motionless and calm in the fury of clouds and rain and waves that beat all around it. Evelyn watched, then followed Jaynie, and saw her disappear behind the rock.

"Wait for me!" she yelled.

When she caught up with her, Jaynie had collapsed on the bottom step. Evelyn put her arm around her. "Jaynie, now answer me! What are we doing down here?"

When Jaynie looked up at her friend Evelyn could see that some of the water running down her cheeks was not raindrops. Jaynie sniffed and wiped her nose on the back of her wet sleeve.

"Oh, Evelyn!" She buried her face against her friend's wet slicker. "Look on the other side."

She got up, put her arms around Evelyn, and walked her slowly around to the far side of the great rock. As they stepped into view of the shoreline, Evelyn gasped, her mouth hung open and Jaynie hugged her.

"Oh, no! Oh, my God!"

The two stood there, their arms around each other, their trembling bodies holding each other in the rain and wind.

Floating in the shallows of the rocky shoreline, the body of Liz Beattie rocked up and back, up and back, in the whitecapped waves blowing off the loch. She lay face up, her long white hair entangled with vines and leaves and the black, slimy rot of algae, while the cold rain fell into her open eyes.

"There, there, love," David Macdonald said to his wife after she told him of the tragedy. "I'll be home as soon as I can, less than an hour. Where are the girls now?"

"Upstairs. They were both so shaken when they got back, what with having to call the Beatties and wait around out there for the police, and show them—everything. Oh, David, I feel so sorry for them. Especially Jaynie. She hasn't been sleeping well since she came, you know. Ay, she *says* she does, but I can see the exhaustion in her eyes, and I don't think she's ever completely gotten over her jetlag."

"So are they both resting now?"

"Ay, and I gave Jaynie a sleeping pill, to help her rest more soundly."

Jaynie did sleep soundly.

Until midnight.

Then, because the sedative was wearing off, and the midnight hour was haunting her, Jaynie awoke. Or was awakened. And again, she performed the midnight ritual — the young girl's troubled voice, calling to her, from some haunted depth. A long, drawn-out call, splitting her name into two desperate cries—

*Jaaay-nieee!*

She rose, knelt up in the bed, and faced the

photo of Loch Ferm with its ghostly figure keeping its vigil in the depths of the water, each night glowing with a seagreen light, always partially concealed and partially disfigured by the loch vines and algae.

"Jaaay-nieee!"

She heard the same dream message in the same hollow voice: "All that could be found!" And always she returned to sleep with the mystery of that message evoking her fantasies, but never satisfying her with further clues or some kind of revelation.

This night, with Liz Beattie dead not even twenty-four hours, the voice and the figure seemed more familiar. When the tangled veil of grass and leaves parted over the lips, Jaynie was even more certain. There, on the lower half of the face, the only part that Jaynie could see clearly, was the sly, curled-lip smile that she had seen on Liz. It was that same sad smile that had made her uncomfortable whenever it appeared, and even more uncomfortable when it disappeared, as it did quickly, absolutely, leaving behind those tight, expression-drained lips that looked as if they had never relaxed into a smile at all.

*Jaaay-nieee!*

Now, yes! Jaynie was positive. It was Liz's voice! And mouth!

*Jaaay-nieee! Sleeeeeeeeeep nooooo moooooooooore!!*

Then Jaynie risked it. Calling the apparition by

name, she asked, "Why, Liz? Tell me, Liz, why can I sleep no more?"

*Macbeth—does—murrrr-derrrr sleeeeeep!!*

And for the first time, that horrid, contemptuous smile lasted, lingered—frozen into a demonic grin that faded into the darkness only as the green light faded, and the photo was once again a misty view in black and white. Jaynie lay back down, a great wave of satisfaction swept over her. She grabbed her pillow in her arms, and finally fell into a sleep that, the next morning, she would tell Mrs. Macdonald was deep.

And restful.

# Chapter Ten

"Did you have any dreams last night?" asked Betty Macdonald, as she placed a heaping bowl of hot porridge in front of Jaynie. Evelyn's mother was getting increasingly worried about the dark circles under Jaynie's eyes. She was on the verge of surrendering her jetlag theory for some other explanation.

Jaynie blushed. "I think I dreamt about Liz last night, but I can't remember exactly how it went." She lowered her head and took another sip of coffee. Evelyn and her parents took the cue that perhaps she did not want to talk about it this early in the morning. Suddenly, Jaynie asked, "Have you ever read *Macbeth*, Mr. Mac?" Evelyn had once told her how her father loved to read the classics and discuss them in great detail with anyone who was interested.

"Ay, Jaynie, a most dreadful story and not one to make the history of Scotland a shining example of enlightened statesmanship, I'll tell you that. Why do you ask?"

"I have to read it next year in English class and I thought I'd read it while I'm actually in Scotland, where it actually happened. It really did happen, didn't it?"

"Oh, yes, Macbeth was the Scottish king back in, I don't know, ten or eleven hundred. He's in the history books, as well as Shakespeare's play. A disgusting fiend, he was. In fact, Shakespeare calls him the 'fiend of Scotland.'"

When David mentioned the word "fiend," some image flashed through Jaynie's memory, an image of something Liz had said the night before she died, when the two girls met in the hall. Something about turning fiends loose? She couldn't remember the exact words.

"What did he do?"

"Well, it isn't a pretty story, lass. Let's just say that he used monstrous means to become king."

"Like what?" Jaynie was getting more and more curious.

"Well, for starters, he was so determined to be king that he murdered the king of Scotland and all other nobles who would challenge his own reign. Nothing would stop him, ay, nothing. He even hired killers to wipe out the families of those who opposed him—women, children, servants, too.

And he used sorcery and witchcraft to do his dirty deeds."

"Sorcery!?"

"Ay, of course!" he chuckled at Jaynie's curiosity.

"So what became of him?" Jaynie wondered out loud.

"Well, after a reign that was marked by ghastly cruelty and even more bloodshed, he—why, did you know that in the history books, it says he grew to like murdering, and *having* people murdered to such an extent that his thirst for blood could not be quenched? Aaah, he was a monstrous fiend, a discredit to the long line of noble Scottish kings.

"Well, there was a prediction by three witches, miserable old hags, they were, that a man, who had not been born of a woman, would one day slay Macbeth. Now, you might be thinking, as Macbeth himself did, that such a prediction could never come true, because where could you find such a man who had not been born of woman? On the other hand, you might conclude that *three* witches can't be wrong." He paused dramatically, his eyes twinkling.

"Where *did* they find such a man?"

"Macduff. On a medical technicality, you could say that Macduff had never been born of woman. Can you guess what it was?" He paused, then continued, "Caesarian birth! Both the history books and Shakespeare claim that Macduff had been 'ripped untimely' from his mother's womb. And to add, shall we say, a pinch of motivation for

Macduff to assassinate the scoundrel, Macduff's *entire* family was one of those that Macbeth had had ruthlessly slaughtered."

"So how did Macduff get him?" asked Jaynie. She was hanging onto every word that came from Mr. Macdonald's mouth.

"Engaged him in a bloody battle for revenge, slew him with a broadsword, severed his head from his dastardly body, and stuck it on a—"

"Daddy!" Evelyn pleaded. "Please, not at the breakfast table." Her eyes were filling up with tears. "The funeral's tomorrow."

"Oh, ay, forgive me, lass. Forgive me. I should have been more conscious of your feelings, more considerate. I'm sorry, Jaynie, I was hoping our Macbeth talk here would get your minds off—"

"Oh, that's all right, Mr. Mac. It's a fascinating story. Do you mind if I borrow your copy to read? I noticed you have Shakespeare on the bookshelves in my room."

"Help yourself, lass."

Again, the conversation dropped off into an awkward silence, everyone lost in somber thoughts about the funeral. Betty Macdonald returned to the kitchen for more muffins. She had always liked Liz, ever since both girls were toddlers. Evelyn kept her head down, wondering how she and Jaynie should spend the rest of this day before the funeral, since neither of them would probably want to do very much, or have to think about very much.

\*     \*     \*

The rest of the day was wet and drizzly. Jaynie called Brian to see how things were going at the Beattie household. He said that his mother was taking it especially hard, but that in spite of the grief that filled the family, the funeral arrangements were coming along as smoothly as could be expected. His voice sounded muffled and lifeless.

In the afternoon, Jaynie and Evelyn took a long walk down the winding little roads that led out of Tweedkeith. They climbed to the top of Ronan's Hill where the summer heather was beginning to come out. They didn't talk very much.

That night, Jaynie went to her room early, and leaning against her pillows, opened the large, dusty volume of Shakespeare and turned to *The Tragedy of Macbeth.*

Scene One was "An Open Place." The stage directions read, "Thunder and lightning. Enter Three Witches."

Jaynie shivered as a cold tingle ran down her spine. Should she begin to read this play tonight? She was tempted to put the book down and turn off the light. But something inside her was curious.

Liz had mentioned *Macbeth* the very first day Jaynie met her. Then she had said something about "turning fiends loose" the night before she died. Then—something in her dream last night— Yes, that's what had been bothering her all day, she realized with a shiver. In her dream last night, Liz's voice mentioned *Macbeth* again. Jaynie closed her eyes and wracked her memory, hoping the words of her dream would come to her again.

No luck. With a sigh of frustration, she picked up the heavy book and she began to read.

First Witch: When shall we three meet again?
In thunder, lightning, or in rain?

Second Witch: When the hurlyburly's done.
When the battles' lost and won.

Creepy, she thought, but continued reading. Her eyes were tired, but something inside her kept nudging her to keep at it until she came across a clue to Liz's mysterious death. She gradually became more convinced that the play contained some shred of evidence or clue that would shed light on why Liz had been so moody lately, and why her death had so many unexplained angles to it. When she came to the end of Act One, she knew she'd never finish the entire play in one night, but she read on to Act Two. She had to get through the scene where Macbeth murders the King.

It was just like Mr. Macdonald had said. An uncontrollable hunger for power, predictions by the witches, bloody daggers. She was wondering how a tale of such violence and immorality could become one of the classics of literature, when she came upon a line that sent a damp chill down her neck and made her shudder. And suddenly, her dream of the previous night burned clearly in her mind.

Oh, no, she gasped. It's here, it *is* here!

Methought I heard a voice cry, "Sleep no
   more!
Macbeth does murder sleep!"

And with that line ringing through her head,
Jaynie's heavy eyelids fell closed, and she slept.
For the first night in a week, Jaynie did not
dream.

# Chapter Eleven

After Liz's funeral service was over, Ian Beattie invited close relatives and friends to join them at the Tweedkeith Arms for tea. Jaynie rode with Evelyn and Craig. When they parked the car and entered the hotel, Evelyn went to the ladies' room. While they were waiting for her to return, Jaynie grabbed the sleeve of Craig's coat and pulled him aside.

"Craig," she began in a low voice, "do you think Uncle Angus would be terribly upset if I talked to him sometime about the legend of Princess Fiona? Evelyn said that he doesn't like people to gossip about it or joke about it, and I don't want to make him mad."

"What do you want to know?" Craig asked.

"Oh, I don't know exactly. I'm just not happy with the thought that Liz died accidentally. And I don't like to think that she committed suicide. If she did, it would be an awfully weird coincidence that two suicides occurred in the very same spot, don't you think?"

"Ay, but what would Uncle Angus know?"

"Well, Liz said something to me the very first day I met her, when she took me down to Loch Ferm. She told me that Uncle Angus believes that Fiona will return someday, and that when she does, it will be for revenge. But you know how he sort of shied away from talking about that when I brought it up at Fermleven the other day. I was wondering if maybe he wouldn't mind talking to me alone sometime."

Craig wrinkled his forehead in thought. "Well, I think if you could get him by himself, especially now, considering the circumstances of Liz's death, he wouldn't mind telling you more about his version of the Fiona legend. You know, there are several versions of it. I've never heard all the details of the revenge part of it." He noted the worried expression on Jaynie's face when he told her there was more than one version. He felt sorry for her and Evelyn. "What are you thinking?" he asked her gently, and put his hand on her shoulder.

"I just wonder if Liz's death had anything to do with revenge."

"Jaynie," he responded skeptically, shaking his

head. "You don't think that Fiona's ghost *murdered* Liz, do you?"

"I don't know," Jaynie said, and went into the pub where the others were gathering for tea, leaving Craig in the hallway to wait for Evelyn.

All day long, Jaynie was trapped in her thoughts about Liz, Fiona, and Macbeth. She felt more and more positive that Liz's mysterious behavior and her unexplained death must have something to do with *Macbeth*, and that a clue could be found in the play. She used the strain of the day's events as an excuse to go to her room. She really wanted to be alone so she could finish the play.

Propped up against the pillows, the little light glowing beside her, Jaynie read through the next acts of *Macbeth* to the part where, as Mr. Macdonald had told her, Macbeth hires thugs to slaughter Macduff's entire family. Being away at the time, Macduff is told by his friend, Ross, what happened at his castle.

Ross: Your castle is surprised, your wife and babes savagely slaughtered . . .

Macduff: My children too?

Ross: Wife, children, servants . . .

And then—the next line made Jaynie's heart skip a beat. She couldn't believe her eyes. She read it

85

again, hearing it in her mind as much as seeing it on the page. Yes, that's what it said! She read it a third time.

Wife, children, servants,

ALL THAT COULD BE FOUND.

She had heard these very words almost every night since she arrived in Scotland, and here they were! The dream message! In *Macbeth*!

Her head was spinning; she felt confused and wanted to know what it all meant. She looked up cautiously at the dark photograph over her bed. The legend of the dead Fiona surrounded her—in Liz's death, in the lines from *Macbeth*, in the photo that possessed some supernatural influence over her dreams. Tears welled up in her eyes as she put the book aside. Her back hurt. She turned out the light and buried her face in the pillow.

"I feel so lonely. I wish Tim were here. No one knows what's happening. I wish I could just go to sleep with his arm around me, and not have to worry about waking up, or dreaming, or anything!" She started to cry and clutched the pillow as tight as she could, and sobbed, "I just want to sleep."

She finally fell asleep. Then, as on other nights, she woke up at midnight and knelt before the glowing photo of Loch Ferm. She felt herself responding to a desperate plea to understand. But understand what?

When the ghostly green light had swelled the figure to its full intensity, Jaynie hesitated a second and then asked in a weak voice, "Are you—? Are you Liz?"

"No, Jaynie. I am not Liz."

"Then who are you? Please tell me," Jaynie begged.

"Jaynie," the wraith spoke slowly, letting each hollow syllable drop into Jaynie's consciousness, "I—was the one—the only one—who could NOT be found."

The ghostly voice paused.

"Jaynie, Jaynie! I COULD *NOT* BE FOUND!!"

The next morning Jaynie slept later than usual. When she went downstairs, she found that Mrs. Macdonald had kept her breakfast hot for her, and had brewed a small pot of coffee, knowing she preferred it to tea in the morning. Evelyn had gone up on High Street to do some grocery shopping. When she returned, Jaynie decided that now, while the two of them were alone in the kitchen, she would ask her friend for advice. She wondered if she could tell Evelyn everything that had been happening to her since she arrived in Scotland? She had to. She couldn't go through all of this alone. She knew she needed help.

"Could we talk about something?"

"Sure," Evelyn said as she began unpacking the shopping bag.

"It's hard to put this into words and make it sound real. I'm just not sure what's real and what's not." Evelyn looked at Jaynie, whose face was drawn. They had been through a lot in the past week.

"What's the matter?"

"First of all, you know how much my dreams affect me." Evelyn nodded. "Well, since I've been here, my dreams are even more powerful and clear every night. In fact, they're getting so sharp that I don't think—I don't think they actually *are* dreams."

"What do you mean your dreams aren't dreams?"

Jaynie ignored the question for the moment. "I wish I could stop thinking about them, but it's impossible." Evelyn sat down in the chair across from Jaynie. "I think that what I remember in the morning is not really a dream, but something I act out, something that happens to me. I can't control myself in my sleep. Or maybe I'm not asleep when it happens. Oh, I don't know. I just don't know." Jaynie shook her head helplessly, wishing that somehow Evelyn would know what she was talking about. She wanted an explanation without having to discuss everything that happened each night.

"What happens to you? Can you talk about it?" It was obvious to Evelyn that something serious was bothering her friend, something more serious than her relationship with Brian—or Liz.

"Well, first of all, every night I dream—no! I'm sure I don't dream it. I think I actually wake up and listen to the spirit of Fiona in the photograph over my bed. She—she—oh, Evie, please don't laugh at this. I'm not crazy. Fiona *talks* to me. And the night after we found Liz's body, the spirit in the photo wasn't Fiona. It was Liz, or someone who sounded an awful lot like Liz."

Evelyn wanted to smile at Jaynie's attempt to unravel her dreams, but she sensed the suppressed panic in Jaynie's face.

"Well, what does Fiona, or Liz, say to you?"

"At first, Fiona just kept repeating one line over and over each night. 'All that could be found.' It didn't make any sense to me. It was just—what we learned in dream club. A cryptic message. I had no idea what it meant. But a whole bunch of things have happened in the last couple of days, and it's almost beginning to make sense."

"What?"

"I'm reading *Macbeth*, you know. And that same line, 'all that could be found,' is in it."

Evelyn's mouth dropped open a little in disbelief. "It is? Where?"

"In the scene where Macduff learns that Macbeth hired killers to murder his wife and children. It states it very clearly—Macbeth's thugs killed *all that could be found*."

"But, Jaynie, that could just be a coincidence, couldn't it?"

"I don't think so," she replied, "because last night Fiona told me something else, something I didn't know before. And I don't think I would have understood if I hadn't first come across that line in *Macbeth*."

"Oh, Jaynie, this is giving me the creeps. What did she say?"

"She said that *she* could *not* be found."

Evelyn frowned. "But what does that mean? I don't get the point."

"Look, Evie, it sounds like she's saying that when everyone else was wiped out, after the killers slaughtered the wife, kids, and servants, or all that could be found, *she* survived."

"Okay," said Evelyn, getting logical, "now let's think this out. We know from the legends that Fiona was a princess from the Highlands, way on the other side of Scotland from Loch Ferm. We know her lover was slain. According to the legends that Craig and Uncle Angus tell, she found her dead lover, kissed his wound, and threw herself into Loch Ferm. But—there's something missing." Evelyn put her head in her hands, thinking hard. "All that could be found, all that could be found." She repeated the line over and over to herself. Suddenly, an idea occurred to her. She looked up at Jaynie. "That's it! That's what's missing!"

"What?"

"Found! Found *where?*"

"On Macduff's estate," answered Jaynie.

"Then Fiona, a Highland princess, was at Macduff's when his castle was raided by Macbeth's killers. And they didn't find her."

"Right."

"That means she wasn't in the Highlands when the murders occurred. She was—" She looked up. "With Macduff. In Fife."

"Evelyn, could all this have happened at—?"

Evelyn cut her off in disbelief. "Oh, my God! At Fermleven?" She bit her lip, pondering the implications, then a puzzled frown crossed her face. "Jaynie, I never read *Macbeth*. Who was Macduff anyway?"

"He was the Thane of Fife," Jaynie answered.

# Chapter Twelve

Jaynie looked at Evelyn nervously. "Come on, Craig said it would be all right," Evelyn encouraged her.

The girls walked up flat stone markers to the low rough porch and knocked on the door. The door cracked open and the old man's face peered out from the dark shadows within.

"Eh?" he asked, half greeting, half questioning.

Evelyn took the lead confidently. "Craig said we could come see you, Uncle Angus. Are you too busy to talk to us for awhile?"

"Talk?" He fired the word at them like a dart. "Talk about what?"

"Jaynie has some—things—to ask you. She has questions about what's been going on lately, like

Liz drowning in the loch." Evelyn tried to tie in the important event of the drowning without alarming the old man. At the mention of Liz, Uncle Angus pulled the door back just enough to let them pass through it, but not so far that it would let much light into his dark little house. The two windows were covered with heavy curtains, and the only light came from the dwindling fire in the hearth, the weak glow reducing what little furniture he had to silhouettes and shadows.

"Actually we came to learn more about the legend of Lady Fiona," said Jaynie.

"And what does Liz have to do with the Fiona legend?" he asked them, making no effort to hide his disbelief.

"That's what we thought *you* might be able to tell us," explained Jaynie. "You see, I've been having dreams about Fiona, and on the very night that we found Liz dead, I thought I saw Liz in my dreams, talking to me from the loch, just as Fiona had done on the other nights."

"Other nights?" The old man sat upright and blinked. "Do you mean you dreamed about Fiona before Liz was—" He broke off his sentence, then corrected it, "Before Liz drowned?"

"Yes, and—oh, please let me tell you everything I know. You believe Fiona will return for revenge against someone, and Liz told me to read *Macbeth* to find out who that someone is. I also know that, or at least Evelyn and I *think* that Fiona must have been engaged to a man here, near Fermleven, if she found his murdered body and then kissed it and immediately threw herself into Loch Ferm. Macbeth's murderers killed all of Macduff's children, and I also read that Macduff was the Thane of Fife, and that Fermleven Manor is in the region that one time long ago was the Kingdom of Fife." She finished her sentence in a nearly inaudible voice, as if afraid that the wrong ears might hear her, would know that she *knew*, that she knew things she shouldn't know.

"And you came here today so that I could tell you that you are right! You have the clues and you needed them arranged, is that it? You have all the pieces of the puzzle except one, and you think that I can supply it for you. Isn't that right?"

"Yes," she said weakly.

Evelyn came to her assistance. "Please, Uncle Angus, what can you tell us that may make sense of Jaynie's dreams, and Liz's death, and all the things that have been tormenting the Beattie family and *us* over the last couple weeks?"

The old man, relenting, began slowly, softly, and not completely unwillingly. "Since you know so much already, I can tell you something that even Ian Beattie and his arrogant preservationists themselves don't know. All of their historical research could trace this place back only to the 1400s. Hah! After that—the *legends* begin, and all we have are the old stories that are sometimes truer and wiser than records and the so-called facts." He grinned at them as he spit out the word "facts." He gazed into a timeless distance, farther away than the four stone walls of the room permitted.

"Promise you will keep this to yourselves, unless it becomes indispensable, or if only by revealing it, you can save yourselves or others." The two girls nodded, mesmerized by the spell his voice cast. "In legend—*legend,* mind you!—this very castle, now called Fermleven Manor, belonged to Macduff, and you're right, he was the master—the Thane of Fife. And what you've come to figure out is that the Lady Fiona was betrothed to Macduff's eldest son who would become the next Thane of Fife. Now, on that ghastly day, Macbeth's hired murderers appeared and savagely slaughtered everyone in the household, but Fiona hid herself in a high turret, in a secret spot behind a fake panel. It's still up there, a part of the castle that was never destroyed. She stayed there, listening to the screams of death, the obscene curses of the murderers, the sorrowful pleadings for mercy that they so ruthlessly ignored. She heard it, she heard it all—she listened as every Macduff—every servant, every maid and workman—was put to the sword! Well, she hid up there for hours, until the killers had left. And when she came down, what did she see? A bloody wreckage, there was! Dead and dying bodies, in the midst of which was that of young Macduff, her own true love. And—" Uncle Angus paused, exhausted — "you know the rest. She kissed the wound on his bloody chest, right over his still heart, and with the taste of his blood on her lips and tongue, she ran from the castle, crazed and half-mad with grief and anger—ay, anger! Down to the loch, she went, where she climbed up onto the great flat rock, kissed it once in farewell, and hurled herself into the deep waters below."

"And she will come back for revenge?" asked Jaynie. She somehow trusted what he was saying as truth.

His voice grew louder, taking on its Jehovah-like tone again. "Ay, that she will! And when she does, we will all—*ALL* need protection. There may not be any of us safe, *NOT ONE!*"

It was obvious to Evelyn as they drove back to Tweedkeith that Uncle Angus' impassioned legends about the dead Fiona and Fermleven Manor had made a deeper impression on her friend than on herself. Evelyn had always thought of Uncle Angus as a clever storyteller and a crafty magician, a bit wild with his herbs and potions and his dabbling in sorcery. However, she never considered him more than a likable, eccentric old man. Jaynie, on the other hand, seemed to have been spellbound by the story of Fiona's future revenge. Evelyn wondered why Jaynie hung on to the old man's words, and why, even though there was no clear connection, she continued to suspect that Liz's death was not an accident, but somehow related to Fiona's legend. Was it because of those nightly dreams? Evelyn was disturbed.

She asked her friend what she thought of

Fermleven Manor being the site of the ghastly murders.

"Oh, it's creepy, all right," Jaynie replied, clenching her fists. She looked out the window over the vast expanse of gray water, and thought for a moment. "I remember a poem I read in a book on Scotland last month while I was getting ready for this visit." She paused, as though she had not been addressing that to anyone in particular.

Evelyn glanced over at her. "How did it go?"

Still there was no response from Jaynie.

"Can you remember it, or part of it?"

"Mmm-hmm." Jaynie sighed wistfully. "It was written in a Scottish dialect which I can't pronounce, but in modern English it went something like this. It's a mother speaking to her daughter.

Go hold your tongue, my daughter dear, be
    still, and be content,
There are more lads in Scotland, you needn't
    so lament.


O there is none in Scotland, there's none
    at all for me,
For I never lov'd a love but one, and he's
    drowned in the sea."

As she recited the verses, Evelyn realized that she was not really thinking about Fiona's lost love, but about her own, about Tim and California.

"Who do you think is right, the mother or the daughter?" Evelyn asked her.

"I don't know," Jaynie answered sullenly, with a feeling of utter helplessness. "I guess they're both right. That's what makes it all so tough. There *are* other boys in the world. I know that. And I also know I never 'loved but one'—and that was Tim—" Her voice trailed off.

"I just don't feel safe, Evie. I mean, I'm having a good time here, sort of, and I like Brian a lot. And you and your parents are wonderful to me. But I feel so alone, and abandoned. I almost feel like Tim is dead, like he died and left me widowed or something. I feel so lonely and angry—yeah, angry." She thought a moment. "So many things have happened since I got here. The car wreck, the dreams, Liz's death, not being able to sleep well at night. I just feel so vulnerable, like I'm losing things, losing control, like I could so easily be—" She groped around for the right word. "Oh, I don't know—raped, slaughtered. Or drowned. Do you know what I mean?" She was pleading now, wanting Evelyn to understand. *Someone* had to understand.

"I think I know what you're getting at," Evelyn reassured her. "In a way you have lost a lot lately, more than just sleep. You lost Tim, at least for now. Who knows what will happen between him and that Julie this summer? You're angry and feel betrayed. You've lost the security of having your family around you. Your friends are back in Ohio. You *have* lost a sense of control over your life. You always do when you're a guest in someone else's home. I felt that way at first when I stayed with you. Other people set the time for this and that, like eating, sleeping, playing, working, you know, all those little things." She reached into Jaynie's totebag for a piece of gum, as she drove down the familiar winding lanes into Tweedkeith.

"You're right, Evie. I really shouldn't expect to be in complete control of myself after having been here such a short time. But why do I feel this way? Why do the unfamiliar things here threaten me so much? After all, everyone has been incredibly nice to me. That's why I can't understand these feelings I get every now and then of wanting to strike out at something or someone. It's like I want to get even—but I'm not sure with whom."

Evelyn was about to suggest Tim, when she let out a sharp cry of pain and pulled her hand out of the totebag. "Jaynie! What's in there?" She felt a sharp, hard, cold object that fit easily into her hand. She cautiously pulled it out of the bag, quickly looked down at it in horror, and then back to the road.

"Jaynie! What are you doing with this?" She was flabbergasted.

Jaynie blushed and took the dagger from Evelyn, shoving it back down into her totebag. "Did you want a stick of gum? I don't think I have any left."

"Well, come on, Jaynie. 'Fess up. What's it doing in your bag? It looks like one of the ones on the wall in your room at Fermleven."

"It is. I went up for it after we talked to Uncle Angus, while you disappeared with Craig to say goodbye. You took longer than usual," she added slyly. Now Evelyn blushed. Jaynie dropped the conversation then, as if her partial explanation made everything clear.

"Jaynie, it's not stealing that I'm worried about. I know you just borrowed it or something, and you'll give it back. But, well, why, for heaven's sake? What are you going to do with it?"

"Be prepared for what Uncle Angus told us." Impatiently, Jaynie glanced over at Evelyn. "He warned us. He warned us, Evelyn! When Fiona returns for revenge we will *all* need protection."

Evelyn shook her head slowly. In the split second before she turned back to look at the road ahead of her, she thought she saw some terrifying expression on Jaynie's face, a look that could be the last desperate plea of an innocent person about to be put in jail, or locked up in an asylum. Or, it suddenly occurred to her, the look of someone crying out for help—to prevent her own suicide.

# Chapter Thirteen

"Jaynie, I've got a message for you," Mrs. Macdonald said when the girls returned. "Brian Beattie called this afternoon and wants you to call him back as soon as you get in." She looked at her daughter and winked.

"I wonder what he wanted?" Jaynie mused aloud. She headed straight for the phone.

"Brian, it's Jaynie," she said when she heard his voice. "How are things?"

"As good as can be expected, I suppose," he said softly. "Mum's taking it very hard, and Dad is his usual stalwart self, not letting on how much he grieves, but I can tell that his stiff upper lip is hiding a lot. He's trying to make life around here as normal as possible, which I guess is the best thing to do. Jaynie, it's awful to suddenly have one less person in your family. It's hard. Real hard." His voice trailed off and there was a long, uncomfortable pause. Jaynie didn't know if she should make conversation or let him continue along the lines he wanted. She waited and bit her lip.

"I know Brian," Jaynie said. "When someone you love leaves you, it's really miserable."

"Well," he began, after a long silence, "I don't know if it's proper, so soon after the funeral and everything. But, Dad thinks it's time for me to get back on my feet and he suggested I go fishing tomorrow. Would you come along with me?"

"Oh, Brian, I really would like to go with you," Jaynie replied. "I'll fix some sandwiches and we can make a picnic out of it. It would do me good, too and there are some things I'd like to talk about with you."

"Oh, that's great! I'll be by to pick you up around ten o'clock tomorrow."

"Brian, what if it rains?"

"It won't! It can't!

"Goodnight, Bonny Jayne, and sleep tight!"

"Goodnight, Brian," Jaynie said softly and waited for him to hang up. When she heard the click of Brian's phone on the hook, she continued to hold her own receiver at her ear, as worrisome doubts flashed across her mind. She was pleased that she had feelings for Brian and he seemed to return them. But was she rushing things, so soon after Tim? And it was so soon after Liz. There were important things to think through before she could feel comfortable with her own emotions again. Maybe she should call him right back and postpone the fishing trip. Up until now, the times she had spent with Brian had been casual and almost always with Evelyn and Craig around. But tomorrow's picnic and fishing trip sounded like it would be a real date, and that scared Jaynie. She wasn't ready for the relationship to turn from friendship into romance. She knew she had romantic thoughts about him, but she just wasn't ready to act on them. And now he seemed to be forcing her to, by asking her out alone on an "official" date. Jaynie felt herself growing angry. Boys are always the first ones to start a romance, and the first to call it quits, she thought furiously. She realized then that she was being a little unfair to Brian and decided that since she had already promised him she would go, she would try to make the best of it. She would let herself have a good time, but she would be careful.

Then, unconsciously, in a nervous motion, she twisted her fingers through the front of her hair, and pulled it down over her face.

"Of course, I'll go with him," she muttered. "It's time." Then she hung up.

Evelyn knocked on the door and stuck her head in, her face glowing.

"How do you feel on the night before your first 'official' date in Scotland? Are you excited?"

Jaynie thought it best not to let Evelyn know how she really felt about the date, since they had had this same discussion plenty of times before and her friend was still convinced of Brian's good intentions. So Jaynie merely smiled and replied, "I've got butterflies in my stomach. It'll be the first time that I've had a date since Tim. And this will be the first time Brian and I have really been alone together since the car accident. It seems awfully soon after the funeral to be running off fishing, though. And going on a date."

Evelyn looked surprised. "You sure don't sound very enthusiastic. I thought you liked Brian."

"I do," Jaynie admitted. She still didn't want to go into the real reasons so she said, "It's just that he must still be really upset over Liz and, and I don't want to seem too happy, or let on that I'm more excited about being with him, than he is with me. In fact I'm not sure how excited I *should* feel."

Even though she thought she knew, Evelyn asked what Jaynie meant.

"Tim. I still feel *something* for him."

"Hostility?"

"Yes, I definitely feel hostility toward him, but it goes deeper than just wanting to get even with him. I want him to know what it feels like to be treated the way he's treated me. I want him to understand the misery and pain he's put me through, even if it means that he has to go through it and feel just as bad as I've felt. Does that sound too horrible?"

"No, I think I know how you feel," said

Evelyn. "But you still feel something for him don't you?"

"That's hard to answer. He's really hurt me, Evie, and I don't think I could ever forget that and just go back to dating him again, even if . . . he wanted to. It's all so confusing! I'm scared I'll *never* get over all this hurt and anger, and I'll never trust boys again. It's a shame, too, because Brian really does seem nice."

Evelyn thought for a moment. "I understand what you're getting at but I think it's time you try to trust again, and Brian's the best person to start with. He really does 'fancy' you a lot. Besides, going out with you would really help him get over this bad time he's going through—you know, Liz."

"Well, I don't want to just *use* Brian," Jaynie protested, "*especially* right now, when he's probably feeling pretty vulnerable."

"I still think you should go out with him," Evelyn said stubbornly. "You don't necessarily have to see it as a date. You can just see him as a friend, but try to keep an open mind about a possible romance. And when the time is right, maybe you can tell him how you feel. Why turn your back on him altogether? After all, you do like him and have a good time when you're with him, right?"

"Yeah," Jaynie answered slowly, "you're right. Well, okay, I'll give it a try."

"Great! Now that sounds like the Jaynie Gerard I know. Well, get some sleep. See you tomorrow."

"Good night," Jaynie said with a smile and

watched her friend leave the room and pull the door tight.

She listened for the sound of Evelyn's door to close. Instead, she heard the water running in the bathroom across the hall. She carefully pulled the totebag out from under her bed and placed it on her lap. She looked at it a moment, then quietly unzipped it and removed the dagger. She held it by its gold handle, blade straight up, and rotated it slowly. She glanced over at the door and pulled the chain to turn off her lamps so that the room was illuminated solely by the gray-blue light from outside. The dagger's silvery blade gleamed like fiery ice.

"It's beautiful," she whispered to herself, mesmerized by the gleam of the blade.

She carefully slid the weapon under her pillow, blade first. Then she patted the pillow down over the handle, arranging the edge of the pillow case, checking to make sure the dagger could not be seen. When she lay down on her stomach, she held her pillow with her left arm and slipped her right hand under the other, testing the position of the handle beneath her head. It was right there. Cool and comforting. Right where she could get it in the night. If she needed it. For an emergency.

She closed her eyes and hoped that a deep, delicious sleep would swallow her and transport her quickly into the next morning when—anything might happen. She was looking forward to tomorrow now that she had talked it all out with Evelyn. She wanted to be alone with Brian to talk to him and overcome her fear of being with a boy again. She felt empty inside, but she knew everything would eventually be all right. She needn't be scared—not of Tim, not of Brian, not of *anyone*. In fact, she thought she understood everything much better now, and that she was ready for anything.

# Chapter Fourteen

"How did you find this secluded spot?" Jaynie asked, with a playful seductive wink as she and Brian approached a dense stretch of forest onto the grassy shore that banked the Tweed River.

"Oh, my dad's been bringing me here for years. I come here a lot when I want to relax and get away from things. It doesn't matter if I catch a fish or not." He laughed.

Jaynie took his arm and motioned to him to be quiet.

"Is that a bagpipe?" Jaynie asked, amused that in such a romantic spot they should catch the sound of a bagpipe wailing in the wind.

"It very well might be. Pipers often come out into the hills, away from the villages, to practice for the summer festivals and parades. If the wind is just right, you can pick up the sound of a piper from miles away."

Brian set his green tackle box down on the grassy bank and began to prepare his gear. Jaynie put the straw picnic basket down on a level spot and spread out a narrow little plaid blanket that Brian kept in the "boot" of the car. She offered Brian a cup of tea from the thermos and they both sat down on the blanket. The air was brisk, the sky sunny, but the British chill hung over the countryside, especially the shady little spot where the two had settled.

Brian sipped his tea and reached for an apple as he stretched his long lanky frame out on the bank. He was obviously not in any hurry to put on his hip boots and wade out into the chilly water. In fact, Jaynie suspected that fishing was just an excuse for an outing in the country, and a chance to be with her, and escape the funereal atmosphere that hung over the Beattie household. She felt sorry for him. She laid down on her back, folded her hands across her stomach and looked up at him.

Eventually, he turned to her and said, "I remember hearing from Evie that you've an American boyfriend named Jim. Right?"

"Tim," Jaynie corrected him, wishing he hadn't brought up that particular topic. "Oh, he's in California for the summer studying architecture."

"And do you still fancy him quite a lot?" Brian asked, although he had heard from Evelyn and

Craig that things were not going well, and it encouraged him.

"No, I think he's interested in someone else right now. Things weren't going very well for us the last month or so, and we'll probably, we'll probably split up for good when we both get back after the summer; I don't think we're still serious about each other."

There, she had said it, and it didn't sound quite as bad as she had thought it would; it also didn't hurt quite as badly. Maybe letting someone like Brian draw it out of her had helped to ease the pain.

"Then your heart's not thousands of miles away across the sea, I take it?" Brian hinted, his blue eyes smiling tenderly at her, and she felt good. She always felt good when his smile reached out and caressed her that way.

"No, my heart's with me. Right here. Pumping like it always does," Jaynie giggled and laid her hand across her chest dramatically, feeling for her heartbeat. "Yep, it's beating."

"Well, does it have a strong and steady beat, or might it be fluttering a wee bit," he asked as he leaned closer to her face. She could feel his breath in her hair. She looked up at the warm affectionate glow on his face, and blushed. He laid his hand across her chest, feeling for the beat. He kissed her on the cheek.

"I think it's fluttering, just a bit, a wee bit," she said as a little laugh escaped from her throat.

She offered him more tea, but he refused and started to unpack his bait. He whistled as he

110

strung his line and got ready to fish.

Jaynie got up and strolled down to the very edge of the water. She felt very comfortable with Brian this morning. As she stared at the changing swirls of color in the water at her feet, she realized that even their conversation about Tim wasn't too bad. It had turned into a conversation about her heart. How sweet of Brian, she thought. He knows how to say things, and let you know what's on his mind, without being obnoxious about it. She watched him pull on his rubber hip boots and stomp down into the water. He smiled back at her as he waded out into the middle of the stream. She smiled and waved, and then went back up the bank a few feet and sat down beside the picnic basket and their gear.

She enjoyed watching Brian cast his line back and forth rhythmically in the bubbling water, the sunlight, every so often, catching on either his belt buckle or an eyelet on the rod. He seemed sure of himself, even though a dark shadow of sorrow across his face occasionally betrayed the memory of what he was going through. Suddenly, without warning, he let out a yelp and tugged on his line. The rod bent like a bow and the line grew taut as it wiggled back and forth in the water, slicing the surface like a sharp nervous knife. Within seconds, Brian had plucked a thick silvery-pink salmon out of the river and held it up for Jaynie to admire.

"I've caught one," he beamed as he held it high in the air.

"Good!" shouted Jaynie and clapped her hands.

"A quick catch!" She watched the fish flop around on the line as Brian opened the little wicker basket at his belt. He dropped it in, disengaged the hook from its mouth, and flapped the top shut.

Jaynie noticed that he did it with the speed and grace of someone who had been catching fish most of his life. I wonder how many fish he's caught altogether, Jaynie wondered as she let her eyes wander around the little clearing where she sat by herself. For a moment, she felt disoriented. Brian was out there in the green water, plucking fish out of the streams and lakes, one by one, locking them up in a basket where they would die. Sealing them, their dead eyes looking up at their captor as the last twinges of life left their bodies, finally seeing nothing, feeling nothing.

The thought of dead fish eyes reminded her of Liz's open eyes the morning they found her. Completely washed up by the waves. Her life washed up.

Cold eyes, green water, green lochs. Fishing. The last time she had been fishing was with Tim. It revolted her. Eating dead fish revolted her. If she could only banish the memory of dead fish, their heads and scales, still twitching with the last fading breath of life, lying helplessly in the basket or on the cleaning block, next to the — A tangle of images confused her thoughts as she tried to remember the tool a fisherman uses to clean fish. That weekend she went fishing with Tim and his friends— What was it they used? She conjured up the image of Tim scraping. She was trying so hard to focus on that day with Tim and see him clearly, that she didn't see Brian anymore in the stream.

She could see a man's strong hand holding the long blade and pinning the fish down on the cutting block with the fingers of his other hand, strangling the fish by the neck, and pushing hard on the blade, pushing it down throughout the skin, the flesh ripping apart. A hand, it was Tim's hand. Tim. She'd show him. She'd get even with him. She heard the horrible crack of the head as it was severed from the fish's body, and saw the dagger all bloody and slimy.

A dagger! It rushed into her mind.

The sharp blue steel of the dagger's blade sliced into the poor helpless creature, doing its repulsive work.

How vulnerable they are! Baited, lured, and caught! And if they aren't perfect for the dagger, they're thrown back into the stream, for someone else to come along and repeat the ancient ritual— bait, lure, catch . . . and kill! She shuddered. Was there no protection for the timid who have no control, the gullible who can't discern the true from the false, the food that gives life from the tantalizing false words of nourishment that conceal a hook, words that flatter and make a woman's heart flutter— What!

Jaynie felt her heart. It was fluttering. She pressed her hand against her chest and gasped in fright. How fast her heart was racing!

And all because of—Brian.

He had forced his hand on her against her will, he had stroked her and asked if her heart was fluttering. And it was! He had caused the rhythm of that flutter, and it was racing, pounding, too fast, and faster, much too fast. She needed air, she couldn't breath—faster—she heard a choking in her throat, and a cry for help was drowned in her lungs before it ever got out.

She needed protection *now*. So, Uncle Angus, this is how it would happen, she thought. She leaned across the picnic basket, grabbed her totebag, and yanked on the zipper. It snagged on the material. I must get it, I must get it, before he returns. She looked up in panic. Brian was turning around and pulling in his line. She jerked at the zipper—stuck! It wouldn't budge. She heard a noise behind her. Then Tim, no Brian, was out of the river, grinning, holding the long rod like a sharp spear, high in the air. She tugged frantically on the zipper. Finally, it ripped loose and she opened the bag the rest of the way, reached in, and fumbled for the dagger. Where is it? The point hooked her thumb and she cried out in pain as Brian stepped up on the bank and stalked up the incline, water dripping from his long rubber-wrapped legs. He was still grinning.

"Help me!" Jaynie cried, fright distorting her face, flooding her eyes.

Brian's smile vanished immediately. "What's the matter, Jaynie?" He dropped his rod and basket and ran the few short steps up to where she was sitting on the blanket, holding onto her hand.

Blood was dripping down her wrist. "What happened? Where are you hurt?"

He took her hand and saw the cut on the tip of her thumb. He quickly stuck it in his mouth, closed his lips around it, and held the base of her thumb tightly between his fingers, pressing it to stop the flow of blood. After a minute, the bleeding had stopped. Brian reached in his tackle box for some first-aid equipment and smiled.

"We seem to be racking up a history of bloody times together. Now I can repay you." He began dabbing alcohol on her thumb. "What did you cut yourself on? Were you fiddling around with the fishing gear? There are a lot of sharp pieces in a tackle box."

"No, I—" She was still shaking. "I cut myself on a pair of scissors in my totebag. I forgot they were in there." She watched him peel open a bandaid and wrap it snugly around her thumb. "That feels better." She noticed the array of first-aid supplies in the box. "I see you come prepared for emergencies."

"Well," he laughed, "you never know when something like this is going to happen. I believe in being prepared. If you don't protect yourself, no one else will, right?"

He looked into her as though he had just read her mind and shared her fear. She recalled Uncle Angus' warning that *everyone* would need protection. But what kind? What kind of protection? Band-Aids? Alcohol? Then a thought, as brief and elusive as the all of one note from a bagpipe in the wind, blew across her mind—show Brian the dagger, so he will know, and prepare himself. *Give him a chance to protect himself. Show it to him!* But the thought vanished quickly.

"What kind of sandwiches did Evelyn's mother make for us?" Brian asked, the emergency apparently over as far as he was concerned. "Are you hungry yet?"

"Yes, you bet I am. I think we have egg salad sandwiches and some meatloaf. With lots of mayonnaise."

She reached for the picnic basket, but her gaze crawled down the shore to where Brian had left the fishing basket with the salmon in it. She thought she heard it flop inside against the wicker walls. Greenish river water was oozing out of the slits in the thatching.

Next to her, in her bag, the silver dagger lay temporarily forgotten, and overhead a large black raven let out a single caw and disappeared.

# Chapter Fifteen

When Jaynie returned Evelyn could tell that things must have gone well.

"How was it? Come on, tell me. What happened?"

"Oh, it was great! I think I *fancy* Brian."

"That's wonderful! He's a great guy for you, Jaynie. But go on! Give it to me blow by blow. But speaking of blows, how did you hurt your thumb?" She pulled Jaynie's white bandaged thumb over for closer inspection.

"Oh, that," Jaynie giggled nervously. "I got a fish hook stuck in it. Nothing serious. Brian whipped out his first-aid kit and just doctored me right up. Can't feel a thing, really." Jaynie changed the subject. "Guess what else? Brian asked me to the fete this weekend at Fermleven Manor. Not just as his date, but to do the kind of hostessing that Liz would have done. Isn't that wonderful?"

"Oh, it is, it is. But you know, this crazy fete is coming awfully soon after the funeral. Won't you feel a bit strange being part of it? I mean, you'll have to spend a lot of time with Brian and his parents, and they're bound to be under an awful strain."

"Oh, I can handle it."

"Are you sure?"

"Of course, silly!" Jaynie bubbled on. "He wants me to come out Friday and spend the night, getting ready. It has to be a really impressive event. Think of all the important people who'll be there—political leaders, ministers, Mr. Beattie's business associates, landowners, even the Laird of Keith. Oh, Evie, I just can't wait. Brian wants me to invite you out Friday night to help out, too. I told him I didn't think I would have to twist your arm very hard."

"Yes, I want to go. I haven't had much time to see Craig recently. I really miss him. But won't you feel sort of strange, having to act like one of the family, substituting for someone who, I mean, won't you feel funny playing Liz's role? You know, a lot of people around here think that the Beatties should call the whole affair off, considering what's happened so recently."

"Oh, but they can't call it off. It's too elaborate. Everything's been planned for months." Then

118

Evelyn noticed an unreadable expression cloud her friend's pretty face.

"Besides," continued Jaynie, in a faint and breathy voice, "I *owe* it to Liz to take her place."

When Jaynie went upstairs to the bathroom to wash her cut and change the bandage, Evelyn stayed at the table, idly fidgeting with her empty teacup. She felt that something was just not right. Jaynie was more sensitive than this. Evelyn wasn't sure quite what to think. She was thrilled about Jaynie finally beginning to feel like she was accepted and feel comfortable with boys again. She remembered how good she had felt on similar occasions after she arrived in Ohio. But something just wasn't right with Jaynie, she was sure of it.

She tried to figure it out. Jaynie had taken Liz's death pretty hard, especially considering that Jaynie barely knew her. On the other hand, she had been the one to find the body. And maybe falling for Brian and sharing his grief added to her own. Then there were her dreams, her restless nights, the long sessions with the police, her loss of sleep over everything. And on top of everything was this anger over Tim, and the possibility of being hurt all over again by Brian, she thought. Jaynie was almost obsessed by it. So much of the confusion centers around boys. Brian seemed both good and bad for Jaynie. And—Jaynie might be both good and bad for him. She doesn't trust him on the one hand, and on the other, she doesn't want to lead him on unfairly, playing on his need for closeness right now. At least she understands that.

Evelyn's head swarmed. It didn't add up. There was some missing factor to explain Jaynie's sudden recovery to her usual spunky self. It wasn't like Jaynie to spring back from the depths of worry so callously. She wished Craig were here to help her figure things out. She needed to discuss Jaynie's recent, strange behavior with him.

As she was about to unpack the picnic basket, Evelyn reached for Jaynie's totebag and dragged it across the table toward her. She glanced out into the hallway and listened for footsteps. It sounded quiet. Jaynie was still upstairs. Then, on a hunch, she unzipped the bag. She noticed the material was ripped. Her hands were trembling, knowing that she was invading Jaynie's privacy. She looked in, noticed a handkerchief with some dried blood on it, and then looked deeper for what she feared she would find. Lying beneath the handkerchief and a wallet, like a slumbering serpent, the sharp blade of the dagger with its twisted handle stared up at her.

On Thursday at breakfast, Jaynie mentioned that she had a dream about Uncle Angus. Betty Macdonald asked her about it, and Jaynie explained that Uncle Angus kept saying that he was the "last guardian of Fermleven Manor."

"What," Jaynie asked Mr. Macdonald, "do you think Angus meant?"

He thought for a moment, and then said, "Well,

Angus' family have been crofters on the estate for many generations, going back farther than even he can probably recollect."

"I wonder how long Angus' folks have been there. How could we find out?" Jaynie asked eagerly. "I mean, if Uncle Angus' family goes back into the early history of Fermleven."

"Ah," began David Macdonald, raising his eyebrows slightly. "You'll want to go to St. Andrew's in Edinburgh where the Scottish Registry is located. Evelyn can take you and you can spend a day there boning up, as it were, on Scottish history."

Jaynie thought the idea to do some research was perfect, especially since she wanted to learn more about Fermleven and she'd be able to talk about it knowledgeably at the upcoming fete. David suggested that a quick way to do that would be to look through Ian Beattie's preservationist data that would also be collected at St. Andrew's. They would have the high points of Fermleven Manor right at their fingertips.

Thursday found the girls in Edinburgh, poring over worn, dusty books and old documents. Evelyn watched Jaynie who was turning pages, running her finger down them, totally engrossed in old names and dates. She watched Jaynie with a growing uneasiness over her obsession for researching Fermleven. She was reminded of Liz's growing curiosity, passion, really over the history and myths of the castle she was working so hard to help restore. But with a pang of sadness and fright, Evelyn quickly pushed any thoughts of Liz to the farthest corners of her mind.

Even at lunch, she couldn't get Jaynie to talk about anything other than Macduff, Fife, Macbeth, Uncle Angus—the whole, long, tangled, mysterious past that surrounded the Beatties' estate. Maybe it was true, as one of their teachers had explained, once a personal interest in the past is established, reading history is more fun than work. Jaynie certainly seemed to be having fun. She was so connected to it that she seemed *driven*.

Evelyn was still trying to get over how different Jaynie had acted since the fishing trip with Brian. She wondered if maybe they had gone a bit farther than Jaynie had admitted, because she really seemed flushed with something—was it love or energy, or enthusiasm? It seemed as if Jaynie had acquired a new self-confidence from a charm or talisman. Or weapon, Evelyn thought, and a lump formed in her throat. She looked fearfully at Jaynie's totebag sitting innocently on the table at her elbow. Was there some unearthly connection between her new confidence and that—? She kept it with her all the time. Evelyn bit her lip and looked back down at her list of families who had been crofters on the Fermleven estate. She was getting tired of research. She wanted to be with Craig.

"Evie! Look at what I found!"

She came around to her side of the table and bent over Jaynie's shoulder. "What's up?"

"I was looking up the name 'Beattie,' just for fun and look what I found?" She pointed to a column of names, printed in an old and faded script, some of them blurred so badly that a magnifying glass was needed to read them. The names Jaynie had her finger on, however, stood out sharp and clear.

"Let's see," said Evelyn, leaning closer. She read the name "Beattie," then ran her eyes down a list of Beatties for several generations back. There were several variations in the spelling of the name, and among them, surprising Evelyn was the name "Macbeattie."

"I'll be darned. Someone in a past generation must have dropped the 'Mac.'"

"But look at this!" Jaynie said, flipping a few pages of the book to the name "Macbeth." Many years ago the name 'Macbeattie' was a variation of the name 'Macbeth.' Do you know what that might mean?" Jaynie looked smugly at her friend.

"Is it what I *think* it means?" asked Evelyn incredulously.

"It could mean that the Beatties can trace themselves back to the clan of—"

Evelyn slowly looked up at her friend as the truth was dawning on her. "Macbeth!" she uttered in a faint voice.

Jaynie's eyes were glued to the page. Evelyn expected her to say something, but she didn't even move. Her eyes were glazed over and her head kept nodding ever so slightly. Evelyn reached over and touched her hand where it lay on the page. "Jaynie." She shook Jaynie's hand but there was no response. "Jaynie, snap out of it! What are you thinking about?" Mesmerized, her friend just stood at the table, bent over and staring at the list of Scottish names, deep in thought, oblivious to everything around her. Evelyn panicked. "Jaynie, come on!" She grabbed Jaynie by the shoulders and pulled her up straight and spun her around so she could look her directly in the face. "Reverie-time's over."

"No, Evelyn, you're wrong. It's just beginning!" Jaynie's voice was cold and unemotional and her eyes were stoney. "And whatever happens to them is deserved."

"Happens to whom?"

"The Beatties. The evil that befalls them is necessary—and deserved."

"Jaynie, stop talking like that!" There was still no glimmer of warmth or life in Jaynie's eyes. They seemed to stare blindly at Evelyn, and on beyond her. Evelyn shook her harder. "Jaynie, snap out of it!"

"I can't breathe!" Jaynie reached for her throat and unfastened a button on her blouse. She pushed Evelyn away. "Let's get out of here. It's too stuffy. I need some air." She turned swiftly, grabbed her bag, and headed for the door.

"Are you all right? You looked like a zombie in there." They were sitting on the steps outside.

After several deep breaths with her head down between her knees, Jaynie sat up, smiled, and said, "I'm all right. Poking around in old historical

124

documents can wear you out." She laughed and Evelyn agreed with her, even though she knew that Jaynie was anything but worn out. In fact, up until the moment she went into her blank-eyed trance, Evelyn had never seen Jaynie with more energy and determination. Something is wrong with Jaynie, she thought, but it's not that she's worn out.

# Chapter Sixteen

The last minute preparations for Saturday's fete wore out all those who came a day early to help. By Friday night, everyone was bushed. The old Fermleven Manor hosted more activity than it had in generations. Caterers were roasting a pig, making hors d'oeuvres and finger sandwiches, stacking plates and arranging silverware; the stable boys had a full house of thoroughbreds, maids and butlers were being coached for what was expected of them the following day; artists and craftsmen had set up their colorful booths on the great lawn. The carnival atmosphere made everyone feel intoxicated.

Jaynie quickly saw that managing a castle

required businesslike know-how, overseeing the hundreds of details and responsibilities. She spent most of the day and the long summer evening with Brian, who was proudly carrying out his father's orders and serving as his stand-in whenever his father was needed in two places at the same time. Jaynie was excited; everyone was. And the excitement swelled as the day wore on.

Finally, darkness fell. The servants and booth-keepers turned in for the night, some to the nearby village, others to vans and tents in an open grassy field near Loch Ferm. Soon the morning would be upon them, and the gala would begin.

When all was done that could be done, Jaynie said goodnight to Brian and looked for Craig and Evelyn, but they couldn't be found. So she climbed the castle stairs and went up to bed.

She wasn't sure what woke her. The clock beside her bed read twelve fifteen. She rolled back over. The castle actually *felt* full, she thought, sensing the presence of others nearby. This night was so different from the last night she slept there—the night she last saw Liz alive.

I wonder if I was the last person to see her alive? she thought to herself, staring up at the dark, high vaulted ceiling.

She remembered Liz telling her that night how the brochure photos would have to be changed to make Fermleven look like the place of tragedy it really was. Liz was right after all, Jaynie concluded. How little I knew that night! So many people died here. All the Macduffs. Fiona. Now Liz. So much blood.

There was something else about blood that Liz had mentioned that night in the hall. How did she put it? Blood is never warm. The blood on your lips, the blood on my brother, the blood on the rock.

The blood on Fiona's Rock.

Jaynie suddenly felt compelled to see if Liz was right.

Now fully awake, she tossed back her pillow, leaped out of bed and pulled on a bathrobe. She found her sneakers and slipped into them, leaving them untied. She grabbed the flashlight from the top of the dresser and flicked it on. The beam of light cut across the room to the daggers hung on the wall. She paused a moment, wondered whether she should take one with her, and decided that she would be safe on her own. Tonight all would be secure, she thought, since the castle and the grounds were bursting with people. She unlatched her door and stepped out into the hallway.

When she got down to the loch, Jaynie shut off the flashlight. People were camped nearby in their vans and tents and she didn't want to disturb them or scare them, or make anybody suspicious. After all, Jaynie thought, I'm hardly a prowler from the village. In fact, considering all the strangers on the grounds, I have more right than they do to be here. After all, I am Brian's friend. Isn't there a chance that maybe, if things work out all right, I might actually visit here often, or maybe one day, permanently?

I do feel like I belong here. This is my place. Brian will be the next Thane of Fife, and this will be my rock.

As she climbed the great slab of granite, a gust of wind blew her long hair over her eyes, a strand of it caught in her mouth and she spit it out. She approached the red spot on the top of the rock solemnly, respectfully, and knelt down to inspect it more closely. The night was silent; she could feel her heart—hear it—pounding in her chest. And the great boulder seemed to pulse with its own life.

*Feel it to see if it's warm or not.*

The rock was chilly in the night air. The purplish moss felt cool on the palm of her hand. Then, she compared the bare spot of the rock with the bloodstain. Ice! The blood stain was freezing, ten times colder than the moss. She felt compelled to test it again—this time with her lips. She bent down so that her lips lightly brushed the fuzzy top of the moss. It tickled her, sending a quiver down her entire body. Then the rock. She pressed her lips firmly on the hard gray surface, lingering as she anticipated her next kiss—in the center of the red stain itself.

She released her mouth from the rock and moved directly over the bloodstain. Her lips parted sensuously as she licked them with the wet tip of her tongue and then, passionately, she pressed them onto the red stain, ignoring the unnatural coldness, as if she were forcing her own warmth into the rock. She had to taste it, she had to know—in her mouth—the feel, the taste of—

Then, without warning, Jaynie felt the presence of someone standing over her. She froze, bent over, her lips and tongue still pressed to the rock. Then she heard distinct footsteps and the rustle of cloth. Out of the corner of her eye, she saw two bare feet, dripping water and covered with a slick green slime, walk slowly around her. She didn't move. She couldn't.

The feet stepped directly in front of her. Slowly, gradually, with the guilty air of one caught in a horrible act, Jaynie raised her head. The feet were those of a young girl, her slim wet legs disappeared under the frayed edge of an ancient white gown, also wet and threaded with weeds— then the hips, narrow, slender, the waist, two thin pale hands dangling from wet arms at each side. Jaynie realized with chilling calmness what she would see as her eyes crept up the figure before her, inch by inch. Horror died and was replaced by a feeling of certainty and rightness. The time had come.

Why wait?

She threw back her head violently, recklessly. "I am here, Fiona. I am here."

She could not see the face, completely masked by long hair, tangled with weeds and vines, but she knew. She had come to know Fiona, to sense her presence, to hear her strangled cries for help.

She had been hearing them from the day she'd arrived. In the day as well as at night. Didn't she understand Fiona's pain and anger at losing her love? The apparition before her did not have to speak. Jaynie recognized the spirit as certainly as she would recognize herself.

"I am here, Fiona," she repeated. "And I am ready."

Then the same voice that Jaynie had come to expect nightly in her dreams, a voice rising from the stale breath of graves where sound is felt, more than heard, spoke to her—

"It will not be easy for you. You love him."

Jaynie nodded and reached out with both hands. The wraith's hands also lifted, like dried leaves gently blown upward in a breeze, and grabbed Jaynie's, the face behind the web of weeds looked down on her, and as they held hands, the voice continued—

"You must help me complete our task. You know why. I have waited centuries—centuries to avenge the death of my own true love. I see his murdered body every night. I cannot sleep and will *not* sleep until his murder is repaid—until these foul, ambitious intruders from the Clan Macbeth are driven from this estate."

"Then—then it's true. The Beatties descend from the Macbeth clan. They are the descendants of the murderers."

"Ay, and it will be a just and fair exchange, these Beattie children for the Macduff children. The girl, Liz, was easy, susceptible and feeble-minded. But Brian is strong. He cannot be lured into the loch as easily. He must be dealt with in other ways. By other means."

"By me," offered Jaynie. "Fiona, it must be me."

"Yes, you are chosen. When Ian Beattie loses two children on these grounds, his beloved Fermleven Manor will become a hideous reminder and the final insult to my lover and his own dead family will be avenged."

"The final insult?" Jaynie's mind lurched as she tried to comprehend.

*"Descendants of Macbeth now own Fermleven!!"*

The voice rose in anger, the words hissed like flames. The rotted weeds dangling before the deathly mouth pulsated with each breath, the stench of death was suffocating.

"Fermleven is the sacred grave of the Macduffs. It must never become the playground for Macbeths! Our spirits must be laid to rest peacefully. Do you imagine our long dark sleep will go undisturbed by these Beatties? Their political friends helping them rise to power? Their acquaintances, riding their horses across these fields, over the skeletons of the rightful owners, entertaining with music and games, turning the shrine of our death into a carnival of insults? Disturbing our eternal rest. Mabeth *still* murders sleep!"

The apparition pulled Jaynie up by her hands, her grip an iron vise. Standing just inches from the decayed odor of the grave, the putrification and slime that hung in front of Fiona's face, Jaynie felt the sensation of nausea rise from the pit of her stomach. But she did not flinch. She knew she had to be strong for her mission. This was her test. She had come so far already, and now the end was in sight. Centuries of injustice would soon be avenged. She had to be strong, for the sake of this dead girl who had chosen her, who had placed *all* confidence in her. Only she could set things right again.

"Fiona," Jaynie whispered, trying to look at the features through the green weedy tangle that hid the specter's face. "Fiona, may I see—your face?"

Jaynie felt Fiona's hand slip out of hers. Slowly, Fiona reached up, her long thin fingers disappearing into the veil of sedge that covered her face. Gracefully, inch by inch, using only her fingertips, she parted the weeds in front of her chin and mouth, and Jaynie could see the delicate lips—still stained with her lover's blood after centuries. Then more! The weeds parted further to reveal her cheeks, pale and wan, sunken below the high skeletal cheek bones. Her wet nose appeared, and Jaynie knew she would see the horror she most feared! *She wanted to see those eyes, desperately, more than anything!*

But before Fiona revealed them, she leaned an inch closer to Jaynie's face, as if one more inch would span the long stretch of centuries, and whispered in her grave-hollow voice, "Jaynie, you know me. You have known me, for a long time. I am, I seek revenge for my slain lover, for my loss and anger. But Jaynie, I am *YOUR ANGER* as well! You, too, know what it is like to suffer in love. *You* know the ache of taunting, restless dreams. *You* know the power of nightmare and the fury of a broken heart. Therefore, *you* will be the instrument of my revenge. Of *our* revenge."

And with that, she pulled the remaining weeds from her face, and, as Jaynie had feared, she was staring not into Fiona's dead, cavernous eyes— *BUT HER OWN!* They were her own tired eyes, sleepless and dark, her own pale cheeks, and her own lips, sad and stained with the rock of death. Her trembling hand reached forward, and she whispered into her own face, "You are my anger." Then she touched Fiona's cheek, and she felt her own cheek touched as by a cold invisible hand. She traced the contour of the face down to the lip, she felt the cold wet blood, still moist, still glistening. As her finger ran down Fiona's face, her own skin tingled in parallel spots, and she felt a finger touch her own lips. She then drew her hand away from the dead girl and tested her own face to make sure. It was there, cold, lifeless, haunting. She put her fingertip to her lips that minutes ago had kissed the bloodstained rock, then looked at it. Blood!

"You are right," said Jaynie with calm resignation. "There is only one anger, and it is you."

"And you?" asked Fiona, a faint smile momentarily melting her icy brittle stare. "Who are you?"

"I am Fiona," Jaynie answered.

When Jaynie awoke the next morning, she calmly cleaned up the small clump of weeds and slime from her pillow, scraped it into a little bundle which she concealed easily in her hand, and took it to the bathroom where she flushed it down the toilet.

# Chapter Seventeen

"The knife goes into the neck, here."

"What happens to the blood?"

"Completely drained out, lassie. Look ye! From the neck into the throat, down the chest to the belly, finally it rips open the groin. One long neat slice'll do it. It all drains out. Ay, there's not much of the insides left when you're through. Then you take the carcass and suspend it from a tree limb by the forelegs, tie it up tight, and just let it hang there until nature and gravity drain it dry."

"But the head and tail, even the feet, are left on," Jaynie observed, fascinated by the process. "We won't be eating them today, so why aren't they cut off?"

"Lass, it's like eating a fish with the head still

on. Mostly for show, you know, mostly for show."
The hired chef smiled at his young interrogator.
"We have to put on a good show for the fancy folk
who are coming today. That's what a pig roast is
all about." He grinned condescendingly, imagin-
ing the fancy and frivolous tastes of the wealthy.

Jaynie saw his point. "Right." At this gathering
you don't just rip open a package of hotdogs.

Evelyn had spent most of the day helping the
craftsmen who had set up booths to display and
sell their wares to the public who would be
attending the fete during the afternoon. She was
hoping she wouldn't be too wiped out to enjoy
herself with Craig that evening when the private
ball would begin for the specially invited guests of
the Beatties. Evelyn was having a splendid time
since so many friends and neighbors from
Tweedkeith had gone up to Fermleven for the
day. She was constantly bumping into old class-
mates, parents of friends, friends of her parents.
Betty and David Macdonald had also come, and
like many of the visitors, they were sporting their
own tartan—that of the Macdonald Clan.

Craig waved from across the lawn and motioned
for her to come up to the house.

"Let's grab some punch and disappear for a
little while," he suggested when she reached the
top of the hill.

"Good idea," she agreed.

"How's Jaynie surviving this 'culture' shock?"
asked Craig when the two had poured themselves

some punch and wandered into a shady out-of-the-way spot.

"I haven't seen her much. I know she spent most of the morning inside, with the cooks. She's been fascinated by the roasting pig. I think Mrs. Beattie asked her to take care of some of the floral arrangements she wanted moved, too."

"I haven't seen Mrs. Beattie all day. How's she taking it?"

"Pretty well, I think. Most people are politely avoiding the topic of Liz."

"And Brian's been charming everyone! He's really more cheerful now that Jaynie is around."

Evelyn thought about that for a moment. "At first, when he invited her to help greet guests, Jaynie and I thought he wanted her to take Liz's place. But the more I think about it, the more I realize that he probably hopes that having Jaynie there will keep people from bringing up the topic of Liz. Having someone who is not a member of the family around gives others a reason to talk about other things, non-family things. Brian's smart indeed."

"It's so soon after the funeral for a festivity like this. It must be hard on the Beatties to have to greet the friends they just received a week ago at the graveyard. It must be fearsome hard on them. But they seem to be holding up rather well. Even Mrs. Beattie. I admire her ever so much."

"I do too," added Evelyn. They sipped their punch for a few minutes and looked at each other. Then Craig said, "You know, you're overlooking the *real* reason Brian wants Jaynie here. He's in love with her. I think he fell in love with her from your letters and when he finally met her he knew for sure."

"I thought so," said Evelyn. "I knew it was coming."

"Ay, that's for sure. I haven't seen him so crazy about anyone since Abbie Campbell, and that was three years ago. All he does when we're together is talk about Jaynie. He's nuts."

"So are you," said Evelyn, pushing him back onto the ground and kissing the top of his nose.

They were silent for a few moments. Then Evelyn asked, "What's Uncle Angus up to this afternoon? He didn't seem exactly thrilled yesterday at the thought of hundreds of people tramping all over *his* estate." She remembered Jaynie's dream in which Angus claimed to be the guardian of Fermleven.

"Oh, he's probably hiding out in his cottage where he'll feel safe from all this. He's in one of his 'castle under siege' moods."

"Why's that?"

"He dreamed about Fiona last night."

"Oh, no." Evelyn's heart sank. She was getting upset by dream talk in general, and Fiona talk in particular. She had hoped that the fete would make everyone, including herself, forget about the dead princess, ghosts and revenge, if just for the weekend.

"Ay, a blamed foolish dream it was. He told me this morning that he saw the ghost of Fiona coming out of the loch all covered with mud and dripping loch water behind her, leaving wet footprints as she trudged up to the castle for her revenge. You know how graphically he describes his visions. What terrified him most was that she had a dagger with her and she was holding it high over her head. He woke up gasping for breath. It really scared him. Once he told me that he thinks Fiona is out to murder *him* for some fool reason that he won't discuss."

"Craig." Evelyn took his hand. "Now *I* just had a vision."

"What?"

"Something that hasn't made a lot of sense. Now I think it does."

"What are you talking about?" He frowned at her as she seemed to drift off into some world from which he was excluded.

"You may not know this, but Jaynie has a dagger. She took one from the wall and has kept it in her totebag since the day we came to talk to Uncle Angus about Liz and Jaynie's dreams. She says she has it for protection."

"Against what?"

"Well, I've been assuming it was to protect her from Fiona. She said that Uncle Angus, and this is true, warned us that *none* of us would be safe when Fiona's ghost returns for revenge. It sounds crazy, I know."

"I don't know much about ghosts, but it seems to me that you can't hurt a bodiless spirit with a dagger. There's nothing to stab."

"Craig, don't you see what you've just said? Jaynie's no fool, either. You don't arm yourself with a medieval dagger to fight off ghosts."

"Then what does she have it for? What's she so afraid of?"

"I think I know, and I think we ought to go find Brian and talk to him about it."

"Why Brian?"

"Because I think, if I'm reading all this correctly, that Uncle Angus has nothing to worry about. It's Brian who isn't safe."

# Chapter Eighteen

They found Brian and managed to pull him away into a small carriage house, in back of the conservatory.

"This won't take long," said Evelyn. "We've got to talk about Jaynie, and I'm not sure it would be good if she saw the three of us together right now."

Brian stared at her uncomprehendingly and said, "Why, she's all right. She's a big hit. Everyone's been asking who she is. Of course, they also want to know what romantic implications there might be, but I'm not saying."

Evelyn cut him off in the middle of his boasting. "Brian, this may be hard to explain to you, but there's something not *right* with Jaynie."

"Not right? What are you talking about?"

"Well, this might sound crazy, really off the wall, but you've got to listen to me. Just hear me out before you say anything. First, one question. Did Jaynie cut herself on a fish hook the other day on your picnic?"

"No, she cut herself on a pair of scissors in her purse."

"Brian, Jaynie doesn't carry scissors in her bag. She has a dagger that she keeps with her. She took it from the display on the wall in her bedroom on the very day we came out to talk to Uncle Angus about Liz and the Fiona legend."

Craig explained. "Uncle Angus told her that we would all need protection from Fiona, but Evie and I were trying to figure out what good a dagger would be against a spirit."

"In other words, Brian, she doesn't have that weapon for self-defense. She's planning to use it on someone."

"Who?"

"On you."

Brian laughed nervously. "Oh, come on."

Evelyn continued. "Now just listen to us, okay? Almost every night since Jaynie has arrived here, she's dreamed that Fiona talks to her from the loch. On the day Liz died, the voice from the loch was Liz's voice. Another thing. Jaynie is reading *Macbeth* because Liz told her the first day they met that if she wanted to know who Fiona was coming back to get, she could find the answer in that play. Well, now Jaynie thinks she knows who Fiona is, and I suspect she not only knows who the next victim will be, she also knows *why* and *how* it's going to be done."

"And you think *I'm* the next victim? Who was the first?"

"Liz."

"Liz? What on earth are you talking about?" Brian was getting angry.

"Because of an unbelievable series of events that may be hard for you to accept. Please, try. Listen to me. The legend claims that Fiona will return to avenge her slain lover. Do you know who that lover was? Young Macduff, slaughtered along with his mother and other brothers and sisters. The servants, too. They were all killed by Macbeth's hired thugs. It's in the history books and the play. According to Uncle Angus, Fiona hid in the castle and escaped being murdered with the others. When she came out from her hiding place and saw the dead body of her lover, she kissed him and drowned herself in Loch Ferm. You know that part of the story. She's supposed to come back to kill off the last descendants of the Macbeth Clan. That's the only way her anger will be appeased." She paused, letting this information sink into Brian's mind.

"And who are they?" he asked her.

"With Liz dead, there's only one. You."

Brian wrinkled up his face in disbelief. "Wait a minute, just hold on. We're not descendants of Macbeth."

"You may *not* be," Evelyn assured him, "but

Jaynie knows that your family name was one time spelled with a 'Mac'—Macbeattie. And she also discovered at St. Andrew's a couple of days ago that 'Macbeattie' is an ancient and little known variation of 'Macbeth.'"

"But Dad tried to trace our family's clan back and there aren't any reliable records before the early fifteen hundreds."

"I know, I know. And I also looked into my Dad's history books and it says that Lady Macbeth had no children. So *you* know, and *we* know that you're not a Macbeth. But as Uncle Angus would say, the legends may be more important than the truth. Jaynie *thinks* you are a Macbeth, and who knows what Fiona thinks! At St. Andrew's, Jaynie freaked out for a few minutes like she'd seen a ghost, and said something about how the evil that has befallen your family is *deserved*. I guess she means Liz. Maybe even the car wreck. And maybe some horror still to come."

Something didn't make sense to Brian, even though he was trying hard to follow Evelyn's logic. "Okay, okay, let's say Fiona is after—" He threw his head back in exasperation and rolled his eyes. "—I can't believe we're standing here talking about a ghost as if she really existed, and was some kind of a threat."

"Well, we are," said Craig. "If your life is in danger, let's talk about *anything*, no matter how unbelievable, so that you'll be safe."

"Have you talked to your uncle about this?" he asked Craig.

"No."

"Look, Brian," said Evelyn. "Uncle Angus had a dream last night that Fiona had returned and was carrying a dagger. We know that Jaynie now carries a dagger. And," she emphasized the next point with added seriousness, "there's something that's been going on right in front of our eyes, and you two haven't noticed it."

"What?"

"Have you noticed how bad Jaynie looks? Brian, I know you think she looks great, but she doesn't. There are dark circles under her eyes, her face looks drawn, she's nervous and shakes a lot. Maybe you can't tell, but I lived with her for a year. I *know* that something is wrong. I can see it. She looks pale and tired, and it seems to get worse every day. Another thing. If you watch her closely, you'll discover she's just putting it on— faking it. She can do that for a day. I'm talking about getting along with you, with *us*. Even after meeting all of you as often as she has, she told me the other night that she doesn't feel she's really in control of herself. In fact, her words were that she was *losing* control." She looked at both boys standing there in front of her, listening to every word. "Do you know what I think?" She paused and looked down at the floor. "I think that Fiona or Fiona's spirit, or something or *someone* is *using* Jaynie. I think she's possessed." Evelyn looked up at Brian. There were tears in her eyes. "Jaynie's been my best friend, and she's slowly drifting into,

I don't know what. Into something that I don't understand, and don't recognize as Jaynie." Craig put his arm around her.

"What can we do?" asked Brian feebly, his voice barely above a whisper. It was dawning on him with shattering clarity what Evelyn was talking about.

Evelyn went on, "Let's assume that Jaynie is possessed, or inhabited by Fiona. I mean, Fiona's *spirit* is somehow using Jaynie, and she's going to use Jaynie to hurt or even kill you, Brian. Now if we assume *that*, no matter how outrageous it seems, what should we do next? Where do we go from here?"

"Confront her with it?" offered Craig. "Make her realize what's happening?"

"Ay," added Brian, "and let her know that *we* know. That may somehow weaken her, or even"— he didn't like to say it—"drive Fiona out."

Evelyn nodded. "Yeah, I think the dangerous thing to do would be *not* to let Jaynie know that we suspect she's up to something. If she needs help, she might not be able to reach out for it unless we make the first move. If she is *beyond* help, then—"

No one completed that sentence. They all sat there in silence for several minutes. Finally, Craig broke the tension.

"We're letting our imaginations run away from us. We really don't know what's bothering Jaynie,

147

and *that's* what we've got to find out. We've got to talk to her."

"You're right, but it can't be me," said Evelyn. "She's already lied to me about the fish hook."

"It must be someone she trusts," said Craig looking squarely at Brian so that he would get the point. "Trusts, or for whatever reason, someone she would be willing to talk to about all this, for *whatever reason*."

When Brian got back to Jaynie, his father had just introduced her to a member of the British Parliament. "Come over, Brian, and help Jaynie out with this question about American lawyers and British barristers."

Brian watched Jaynie as they chatted about the difference in the legal systems of the two countries. She smiled just as she always did around him. Nothing seemed out of the ordinary as they finished up one conversation with a guest and drifted into another. If not for the meeting with Evelyn and Craig, he would have enjoyed the rest of the afternoon, but now he found himself watching Jaynie, spying on her when he thought she wasn't aware of him, keeping track of any expression or mannerism that seemed odd. For the most part, he thought, she was cheerful. In fact, if there was something different about her, it was that she was *too* pleasant, too consistently pleasant. Even Jaynie, who seemed naturally happy, would occasionally slip into a melancholy mood, allow a frown to cross her face, especially when someone said something which she found disappointing or about friends hurting each other. But today her smile was like a mask. It seemed frozen. Eventually he even noticed that she didn't have a special look for him. It was as if she had painted her smile on for the day and couldn't vary it.

By evening, Brian had come to the conclusion that Evelyn might be right. Jaynie wasn't herself. She was like a robot full of empty cheer for everyone—stranger and friend. And nothing special for Brian. Brian resented her treating him exactly as she was treating newly arrived guests whom she had never met before. Jaynie was definitely not herself. Something deceptive and evil was definitely dwelling inside her.

Tonight, Brian decided, I've got to talk to her.

As she stepped up to the buffet, he snatched her arm and gave it a friendly squeeze.

"Bonny Jayne, I'm getting tired of sharing you with so many folks all day. How about a rendezvous later after they all leave?"

Jaynie's eyes flashed brightly at him as she exclaimed, "Oh, yes. Let's go off by ourselves for a while. I'm really getting tired of being with people I hardly know." She does look tired, thought Brian, and drawn, just like Evelyn described. He looked into her eyes and at the little lines at the corner of her mouth. It was like looking at two Jaynies: one who was gracious and bubbly, and another, hiding behind the filmy cheerfulness, who was weak and vulnerable and very, very tired.

"How about up in the turret? We'd get a great view of the moon."

"No, I'd prefer down on the loch a little after midnight," she suggested. "It'll be dark then and everyone should be gone. We could climb Fiona's Rock and watch the moon rise over the water. Won't it be full tonight?"

"Ay, it will. The loch then, at midnight."

"That'll be *perfect*," she said, and added, "Do you think it would be all right if I take a little nap before we go down to the loch? I wouldn't want to fall asleep on you later." She smiled directly at him, and he looked away.

"Sure, take a rest. You've been working hard all day." He gave her a quick kiss on the cheek, from which she recoiled with a snap. For the first time all day, Jaynie's face lost its glow. Brian pretended not to notice. "See you at midnight," he said.

Jaynie was grateful to finally slip out of her long yellow dress and drop onto the bed. It felt so good to close her eyes and relax, to push the day away.

A slightly drunk male voice downstairs shouted, "Where's my wife?" and a car door slammed. "I'm here, dear," a woman answered, her shrill voice lost in the chatter of other voices.

This brief snatch of conversation, mumbled in the breakup of farewells below her window, re-

minded Jaynie of the line from *Macbeth* that had
been haunting her all day—

The Thane of Fife had a wife. Where is she
now?

Dead, she thought, drifting off into sleep. All
murdered. Except for me.

# Chapter Nineteen

Brian's long legs carried him briskly down the lawn to the pine woods. A large full moon rose over Loch Ferm. The night was exceedingly calm, forbodingly quiet, especially now after the guests had left the manor; the only sound was Brian's determined running. When he reached the wide clearing, he stopped to catch his breath and look around. The steep hills across the silvery water looked soft and gray. On the brightly lit shore, he could see no human figure, no movement, no trace that Jaynie had arrived before him. He hoped she hadn't fallen asleep and missed their meeting. He looked again, up and down the shore, but saw no one. He was alone.

He walked more slowly down to the water's

edge, bent over and touched it with his hand. Cold, almost icy. The full moon's light overpowered a great many stars. How silent and still, he thought. Almost like a tomb, just the moon, the water, me, and he looked down at Fiona's Rock stretching up from the shore, clear and distinctly outlined in the moonlight. And *that!* he said to himself bitterly. What *is* down there beneath that monstrosity? Is there really some evil, some overwhelming force, lurking there, with power to—to destroy my sister and me—and even Jaynie?

Eyeing the rock suspiciously, he moved down to it and climbed up on top, walked over to the edge and sat down with his bare legs dangling over the side. The cliff edge was sharp and scratched the skin behind his knees. He stared down into the dark depths of the water, thoughtfully, skeptically.

This is where the dread Fiona is supposed to dwell, he said to himself, cynically. Murders, spirits, revenge, daggers.

All afternoon and evening he had thought about what Evelyn and Craig had told him, and he was coming more and more to the conviction that there was no Fiona, no spirit, no revenge. There was only Uncle Angus! Uncle Angus and his ghost stories. For some mysterious reason Uncle Angus was at the bottom of all this, he decided. He was using the Fiona legend to fill Jaynie's head with nonsense. He wondered if Uncle Angus might have more power over people's imaginations than they realized. Perhaps he scared Jaynie into stealing the dagger, and then told Craig that Fiona is coming back for revenge. But why? What would he get out of it?

Ghosts, he thought. Spirits. Jaynie. He desperately wanted to see her. He wondered what her mood would be when she arrived. He hoped she wasn't too tired. He had more to talk to her about than ghosts.

Faintly, he heard the measured crunching sound of someone walking down the shore. It got closer and louder. He looked down and saw a tall, slender figure with long hair wearing a loose white shirt. The figure, moving with a quiet grace, appeared to float brightly in the moonlight. It was Jaynie. He stood up to wave, but stopped when he saw her turn sharply without notice, and walk out into the water. She stepped several feet out into the shallows and bent down, plunging her arms into the black water up to her elbows. She was pulling at something, struggling with something, or someone. Brian thought again of calling out to her, but he couldn't. He watched, dumbfounded, as Jaynie stood up to her knees in water and pulled and pulled at something below the surface. A quick thought of Jaynie finding his sister on that dreadful morning flashed across his mind and then disappeared, as Jaynie stood up and raised her hands to her head. Brian stepped over to the edge of the cliff to get a better look down the shore. He stared hard into the night.

Then Jaynie stood straight up, turned, and

continued walking down the shoreline in the knee-deep water, stepping over large stones and around brakes of reeds and fronds that got in her way. She was coming toward Fiona's Rock. Brian could hear the sloshing of her steps as they drew nearer.

When she was about twenty-five feet from the rock, he waved and called down to her, "Jaynie! I'm up here."

She stopped moving and looked up at him silently. He could see the moonlight touching her cheek and shining off the tip of her nose. He noticed her smooth chest where her shirt cupped and caught the shadow. Her eyes were lost in the darkness of what appeared to be a hood, although she wore no hood. But, yes! There *was* something there, swelling the shape of her head, distorting the natural fall of her hair. Brian strained to see into the darkness. Weeds! And leaves! Jaynie had woven a clump of weeds into her hair! So that's what she was doing in the shallows, he thought. But why? A deep feeling of dread traveled up his spine.

"Jaynie!" He urgently called again. She made no reply, but continued standing there, knee-deep in water, silently, steadily, staring up to where he was.

"Don't you want to come up? The loch looks beautiful in the moonlight from here." He had to see her, even as his own fear set his pulse pounding, his heart racing.

Still, no reply. Brian wished he could make out the rest of her features, her eyes and mouth, he wanted, he needed, some indication of her mood. She turned her head slightly away from the moon and the place where her face should have been into a dark, blank void of nothingness, surrounded by the fantastic tangle of weeds and leaves that sparkled wetly in the moonlight. Then she turned completely toward the shore and stepped out of the water, her jeans wrapped in wet wrinkles around her calves. Brian noticed she was barefoot, and he knew the water was cold. He watched her walk slowly around the back of the rock to the steps that led to the top. Still, she said nothing. No word of warning. The sharp rocks on her bare feet did not slow her march toward him.

He returned to the middle of the rocky shelf and watched for her to come up. Then he saw her—first her head, flushed with moonlight, the weird green net of leaves in her hair dripping down her face and onto the front of her shirt, her features hidden. He held out his hand as she mounted the top steps one by one, each step bringing her higher and more fully into view. He smiled. "Jaynie, come here." Ignoring his offered hand, she took the final step to the top of the rock by herself and stood there barefoot, water dripping in puddles around her feet. And still she was silent.

Nervously, Brian pleaded with her. "Please, talk to me."

Then Jaynie broke the silence. *"You* are standing in his blood!"

Startled by her remark, Brian quickly looked at

his feet and back up to confront this reed-shrouded face. "You mean—? You mean the legend? This red stain in the—"

"This *blood* stain!" She screamed it at him. "Blood stain!" she shrieked. "You know that it is *blood. His* blood. Say it!" Her last words echoed across the loch.

Hesitantly, nervously, Brian whispered, "It is his blood."

"Whose?"

"Macduff's?" It was more a question than a statement. Brian didn't understand this girl he loved, only that something dreadfully evil had transformed her into—into something macabre.

"*My* Macduff's blood. Who is no more, who is no more." Her wailing reply seemed to echo from centuries of loneliness and anger.

Brian froze, his own blood felt cold in his veins.

"Step out of his blood," she commanded, and Brian took one step backward, closer to the edge of the rock. He glanced quickly over his shoulder to where the edge waited for him, and then returned to Jaynie. He would try to reason with her.

"Look, Jaynie, it's true he is no more. He's—"

"—dead, murdered—in California." She cut him off.

"What?"

"Do not call me 'Jaynie,'" she said. "Jaynie is no more. She has not existed for a long, long time, but *I* have existed, and waited, for centuries for this night, this final night of revenge."

His hopes sank as he realized that she was not rational. Reasoning would not work, she was beyond it.

"Who—who are you then?"

"Anger! I am the anger that will not forget." She paused a moment. "My anger will not forget the haunted dreams, or forgive the loss of blood and love, and the loss of land."

"What land?" Brian asked, taking another step backward toward the edge of the rock, as Jaynie took one step closer to him, forcing him back.

"*This* land! Fermleven! This land of death, this graveyard where my love is buried. Do you think I will tolerate it falling into *your* bloody hands, Macbeth? DO YOU?" She stepped one step closer her bare toes almost touching the bloodstain in front of her. Her eyes gleamed with an intensity he'd never seen before.

"Look," he pleaded with her, "I am not a Macbeth, Liz was not a Macbeth. My family was not responsible for the blood shed here nine centuries ago. We couldn't possibly be guilty."

"You *are* responsible, Macbeth. Or do you prefer 'Macbeattie'?" She laughed coldly at him. She seemed to be gaining confidence, almost relishing the evil she was there to carry out. "If you don't believe me, will you believe Liz?"

A lump caught in his throat. Did she think Liz was still alive? "What—what do you mean?" he asked angrily, fear beginning to drain what strength he possessed.

"Liz can tell you. She's standing right behind

you, Brian Macbeth. Careful! Turn around slowly, very slowly, and ask her." A low obscene snicker rattled in Jaynie's throat.

Brian turned to look over his shoulder, and as he did, Jaynie's hand disappeared up under her wet shirt and swiftly pulled out the dagger. Holding it high above her head, she stepped forward onto the bloodstain.

"Jaynie!" he cried out.

Then he spotted the dagger held high above Jaynie's weed-wreathed head. Her hands clutched the weapon in a white-knuckle grip, its blade gleaming between her arms and pointed downward at him. She stood only a few paces in front of him, and he one short step from the edge of the rock behind him, and the deep water below.

"Oh no!" he moaned, as the thought of death became more real. "Where did you get that dagger?"

"I *carry* it always," she replied sarcastically, raising it a few inches higher with a swift upward jerk, her tongue licking her lips, savoring Brian's terror.

"For protection?" he asked, remembering what Evelyn had told him earlier.

"NO! Of course not!"

"But Uncle Angus said we would *all* need protection from Fiona when she—"

"*I* do not need protection from Fiona." Her voice snapped back, outraged by his insult.

"But she will return for revenge," Brian continued, playing for time.

"A revenge soon to be completed. Very soon. And quickly. Liz was no problem, you know. She was already far gone. She was weak. She was *easy*." The slight bend in Jaynie's arms disappeared as she stretched them their full length above her head.

"But what will it get you? More murder will not bring back your loved one."

"No, but it will return this land to me, and to all who are buried here. I imagine your father will sell it rather quickly, Macbeth, when he finds his young handsome son where he found his daughter." She stepped closer to him.

"But is that *all* you want?" he shouted.

He closed the remaining space between them, as he reached up and grabbed her wrists in his hands, just as she leaned backward to add her complete force to the fatal plunge of the dagger. He could feel the strength in her arms pushing downward, struggling. It was not Jaynie's strength, it was stronger, an inhuman strength. He realized that the wrists he held were not Jaynie's. He could clearly see the uncontrollable rage in her eyes, it was not Jaynie's, or Fiona's alone, but the universal rage of everyone whose love had been unforgivably violated.

Still holding her wrists tightly, and resisting her downward pull, he softly repeated, "Is that *all* you want?" He stepped so close to her that she could feel his chest press against her wet shirt, his lips only a hair's breadth away from her own. He locked his eyes with hers, pleading with her to hear him and understand him.

"Fiona," he began, his voice a seductive, breathy whisper, his lips almost brushing hers. "Go ahead and kill me. Repeat the tragedy of murdered love. And you can return to your grave, down there, and be forgotten, be lonely. Or, kiss me and be mine. For I love you, Bonny Jayne, I truly do."

She threw her head back and shook it violently. A clump of weeds fell to the rock. Her lips parted as she opened her mouth like a wild, crazed animal about to howl its fury at the moon and sink bared fangs into its victim. Her arms tensed upward, and she brought her mouth down on his, hard, and he felt the cold, sharp animal teeth of Fiona bite into his lips and draw blood . . . and then, relaxing, melt into the sobbing, uncontrollable kiss of his Bonny Jayne.

"Oh . . . oh! I care for you too, Brian. Oh, thank God! I *do* love you!"

Trembling, her hands slid down into his, and, as he slipped the dagger from them, her arms fell around his shoulders and hugged him . . . and he held her.

# Epilogue

When Jaynie woke up the next morning, she saw Brian sitting on the edge of her bed, looking at her tenderly.

He kissed her forehead and she opened her eyes wider. He smiled down at her.

"Are you all right? You look good and rested."

"How did I get here?" asked Jaynie, pulling him toward her in a great big hug.

"We brought you here last night. Do you remember?"

"Mmmmmm," she said. "It was wonderful!"

"Wonderful?" Brian's mouth fell slightly open.

"Sure! You said you loved me. And I love you, too. I told you so and I still mean it."

"But, Jaynie, what about, all the rest that happened?"

She closed her eyes, sealing out his persistently inquisitive glance. She took a deep breath, held it a second or two, and exhaled loudly. "Well, I *am* a bit embarrassed. I guess I was just overly tired."

"Tired?"

"Well, falling asleep like that while we were down at the loch. Oh, but the moon was gorgeous, and, and it was a perfect, no, almost magical, ending to a spectacular day!" She looked into his eyes innocently, no trace of deception clouded her face. She certainly sounded convincing. "I really loved it, Brian."

Perhaps Jaynie really didn't remember the horror of last night, he thought. Then there was a gentle rapping at the door. Immediately, it popped open and Evelyn came in with a tray of mugs.

"Hi there, sleepy-head! I heard you two talking from downstairs. I decided to barge in and bring you some—"

Jaynie interrupted her. "Make mine tea, Evie. I feel like I should be a tea drinker this morning. No coffee for me today.

"By the way, did Craig come back here too?"

"No," Evelyn replied, "but he called a little while ago. He said Fermleven is back to normal, and it seems Uncle Angus has calmed down too. Now that the fete is over he's accepted that sharing the estate with outsiders won't be so bad. He won't be as protective now, Craig's sure."

Brian shook his head in disbelief. "All those spooky stories and everything. He's certainly a character. Maybe he'll take it easier now."

Jaynie sat up in bed and took the cup of tea and began to sip it slowly. She noticed both Brian and Evelyn observing her with concern. A faint twinge of memory surfaced.

"Brian, I have this feeling that something happened last night I should be embarrassed about."

"Maybe *you* should tell *us* what you remember," Brian began slowly. "Do *you* remember anything wrong?"

She stared into her cup and thought a moment, her reflection in the tea reminded her of— Then she looked up onto the wall, where the photo of Loch Ferm had been, and noticed it was gone. Startled by its disappearance, she turned to Evelyn, questioningly.

"I took Liz's pictures down this morning while you were sleeping, Jaynie."

"Then—" Jaynie stuttered over her thoughts. There was something she couldn't remember, and didn't want to remember.

"Then, Fiona's gone?" She turned to Evelyn for reassurance. "Is she *really* gone?"

"The photos are gone, Jaynie. I stored them away in my room."

"But Fiona," Jaynie continued, pressing for information, for a word, an image that might crystallize her own thoughts. "Is Fiona gone? I've been so terrified about the legend that she will return. She will, you know, I think Uncle Angus was right. We all need protection from her."

Oh, no, thought Evelyn, when she heard Jaynie

begin her talk about protection again. "What do you mean?" she asked warily.

"Because, I've thought a lot about Fiona since I came here. Actually, I've been obsessed by her. I even started to, well, I felt I really *knew* her. You know that, Evie, I talked to you about it." She turned to Brian. "Brian, I used to dream about Fiona almost every night, and I think I understand—I mean, I know how she felt when she lost Macduff. I can sympathize with her. She lost someone—someone she really loved." The words came out slowly. "I think I was afraid of her because I knew how easily I could become like her, angry and lonely. I really felt betrayed and I understand what it is to want revenge. I felt that I needed protection. Protection from myself and my worries. Even from you, Brian, from falling for you. I didn't think I could handle it. I was afraid to trust you. But I don't feel like that anymore because, well, because I believe that you really love me." She smiled at him and reached out, throwing her arms around his neck. "I think, when you told me last night, you saved me from being hateful. You saved me from wanting to get even with— Let's just say I don't need to get even. I don't need to destroy the past. I can just forget it."

Listening to all this, Evelyn wondered whether Jaynie was speaking completely honestly, could this really be all Jaynie remembered about the previous night, and the last few days? Had Jaynie repressed, or forgotten, all the horror they had been through? Evelyn wanted to ask directly about the dagger, the attack on Brian, Jaynie's acceptance of the Beatties being descendants of Macbeth; but she didn't want to call up the dreams, the spirits, the anger that seemed to have been laid to rest. Carefully, she tested her friend. "Do *you* think Fiona is truly gone, Jaynie?"

"Oh no, Evie. Fiona will never be gone. We may still dream about her. There's something universal about her, I think. She may haunt us the rest of our lives. She'll always be a presence because there are things to be angry about. But there are ways to control those feelings too." Evelyn nodded.

Jaynie smiled at Brian. "Brian, if you only knew how obsessed I've been with Fiona. Evelyn knows. I *have* been dreaming about her every night, and I'm sure I know why. Miss Kurzberg, she's our psychology teacher at school, says that when you dream, you're always dreaming about yourself, your problems and worries, things you're trying to work out during the day and can't find answers for. You still think about yourself at night, only in dreams you or the dilemmas become distorted and grotesque. But no matter what you see in your dreams, Brian, it's you, in some shape or form. I did an awful lot of horrible dreaming about myself these last few weeks." She sighed. "*Now* I'm going to start dreaming about you!" She kissed him tenderly on the lips and he held her tightly.

"Jaynie, whatever happened, we've got each other now, and nothing's going to come between us. That's what really matters." Brian squeezed her hand.

Evelyn looked at Jaynie's happy, well rested face. She knew everything would be all right. As Brian pulled Jaynie toward him for another embrace, Evelyn collected their mugs and went back downstairs for refills. She had a strong feeling that Jaynie had said her last words about Fiona. Perhaps they would never know exactly what Jaynie actually remembered, but it didn't matter. Evelyn filled the three mugs and started up the stairs. She felt more relaxed than she had all summer. When she reached the landing, she noticed how quiet it was in Jaynie's room. She waited a moment to see if Brian or Jaynie would call to her to hurry up.

When they didn't, she sat down on the landing, stretched her legs out, stirred her tea, and drank it slowly.